Boy Brainy

JENNY O'BRIEN

All of the living characters in this book aren't real! Any
similarities, herein are purely coincidental. All of the other historical
people in this book are real, except for the ghost of King Arthur -
Ghosts aren't real, but don't tell Arty – he might get upset!
Conwy Castle, Conwy Library, Edwards of Conwy and of course
the Co-op all exist, all other places, and indeed the people that work
there are entirely imaginary.

An apology
The weather in Wales is much better than Jen makes out!
The Conwy Visitor Centre doesn't stock 'Pretty Ugly Pottery.'
Sadly this range is no longer available.

DEDICATION

To Alan: Thank you for trying to keep my feet on the ground,
while my head has been escaping to the clouds.

CONTENTS

ACKNOWLEDGMENTS

Thank you to The Gwenllian Society for all your help and
support

DAI

I'm Dai. No, not dead: Dai - although dead is what I'll be if I can't find that shoe. I'll be pulverised like plasticine by Greasy Guillim if I have to go to school in my trainers again. Not that I can find my trainers either - I think they've decided to hide out and party with the rest of my footwear, but where? That is the question.

My eyes are drawn to the shoebox in the corner, even as I struggle to avoid the elephant in the room. Well it's not actually an elephant. Who'd have an elephant in their room?

No, it's a panda. But not just one panda – two! Two pandas I'll be forced to wear on my feet, if I can't come up with an alternative pretty quick. They're still brand new, and that's the way they'll remain if I've anything to do with it. I know Granny Paddy's old, but that's no excuse for furry animal slippers at my age.

As panic starts to squeeze, tighter than a snakes' embrace, I glance around my room in an effort to work this out logically. It has to be somewhere, unless a ghost has materialised during the night and spirited it away, and that's not logical.

Where is it?
On the bed? No.
In the bed? Nooooo.
In the shoe basket? – not a hope!
In the laundry basket?

I throw a glance at the pristine white box. That's what the floor is for – right?

On top of the wardrobe, which I can just about reach if I jump on my bed and bounce with all four stone of me?
Phew! I heave a huge sigh of relief at seeing the heel of my shoe nudging up against my beaten up old trainer.

'On top of the wardrobe?' you might be asking *'How on earth did your shoe get on top of your wardrobe?'*

Well, did you see that goal last week on the telly? You know the one? The one where Sanchez O'Hoolihan did a double back flip to lob the football in against Man U in the last thirty seconds and go on to win the F A cup. No? Shame. Now if Mum would only allow me balls in the bedroom I wouldn't have to resort to shoes, would I?

So now you know my first name, you might as well know the worst. My name is Dai Monday. I know, it sucks, doesn't it, but it's the name I was born with, so show some respect. Dai after my Great Great Uncle Dai, just in case – just in case he left me anything in his will: mercenary, but effective on the parent front. Although they probably meant some money to accumulate, on a fixed interest rate for my college fund, and not the unique set of toasting forks that arrived shortly after his departure to pastures new.

Toasting forks that were the bee's knees for making marshmallows drip in front of a blazing coal fire. That is unless your dad ripped yours out years ago in favour of a three bar electric version. There are still traces of singed pink goo on the side of the element Mum couldn't quite reach with the scouring pad.

I slip my shoes on and wonder would things have been any easier if old Uncle Dai had been called something ordinary? You know, like Mark or Simon, maybe? I'd like to think so, but blaming someone else for my problems isn't going to make them disappear. Anyway, for all its faults, I'm actually quite attached to my name. It certainly scares the neighbours when Mum shouts me in for my tea!

It's a good job I do have one friend, even if Winthrop does seem to be as unpopular as me. Being unpopular with a friend isn't quite as bad as just being unpopular, but it doesn't stop the bullying. It just means there's someone to compare bruises with, someone to share hiding places with and someone to help invent excuses to put worried parents off the scent.

Win and I live next door to each other, we've always lived next door to each other and we've always been mates. He's forever scrambling over the half bald hedge, which separates our back gardens, to play footie. My mum doesn't mind and he doesn't have a mum to mind; she died when he was born.

2

They used to live in Jamaica, but his dad decided to move when Win was still in nappies. Win's dad is now a fireman, which is way cool. My dad, on the other hand, is an accountant...

Win lives at number twelve Coconut Clos and I live at number eleven, or the hairy house as it's more commonly known, thanks to the previous owners' love of Ivy. There are probably thousands of similar Clos across Wales – you know the sort: sixteen houses, fourteen dustbins, eight lampposts, six cats, four dogs, three rabbits, two budgies, one canary, one bully and an alligator (inflatable). All of the houses are the same: semi-detached with shared driveways and three bedrooms, or two bedrooms and a box room.

Yeah, you guessed it - I have the box room. I don't know why they called it that. It's not cube shaped and there isn't a box in sight, although my mum often screams up the stairs at me to put a lid on it if my music gets too loud.

You can always tell someone's worth by the size of their space: in my case three metres by two metres and ten centimetres says a lot! I live with my mum and dad and big sister, Sammy, who smells. Sammy's fourteen, and is three years, fifty one days and twelve hours older than me. She lives in the second largest bedroom (four metres by three metres). She's cool most of the time, even though she has a larger bedroom and yucky taste in perfume. Only last week I got into mega trouble on the perfume issue. Being me means being clumsy, it comes with the territory. Mum is forever telling me to be more careful, but don't you think I would if I could?

It's just that things seem to happen whenever I get close, and not for the better. Last week I was playing in the bathroom and I knocked over Sammy's jumbo bottle of SmellALot. The one she's been saving up for ages from her Saturday job working for Mr Lloyd. Not only did half the bottle tip out, it tipped out all over Granny Gosh's old dresser. I would have topped it up with water, but it not only smelt horrible - it also stripped varnish off furniture! Mum cried, Sammy screamed and Dad looked on the internet to see if he could patent SmellALot as a paint stripper. Much later, when Sammy had stopped ranting, Mum held both my shoulders so I couldn't avoid her eyes.

'I know it's not your fault you're so clumsy, but please try to be more careful.'

Her voice was the quiet one – the one that means she's really upset. I much prefer it when she shouts.

'Dai, it's time for breakfast.'

Speak of the devil. If she didn't already have a job she could always set herself up as a fog horn.

It's not that I'm clumsy exactly. Well I am clumsy, but clumsy for a reason if you know what I mean. I've got this thing they call Asperger's, which means I'm usually thinking about something more important than where my arms and legs are. Talking of arms and legs I suppose you want to know what I look like.

'Dai, your breakfast is on the table.'

You could say I'm short (one metre and twenty six centimetres), but height is relative, isn't it? Compared to an adult I'm a titch, but when compared to the other ten year old boys in my class, I'm the twentieth tallest, or sixth shortest, depending on which end you're looking at. Win is three centimetres taller than me and never lets me forget it.

'Dai, hurry up! We have to leave in fifteen minutes.'

My hair is red and straight, very ordinary and not very stylish. I have blue eyes, nothing special, except that they don't work as well as they should, hence the geeky glasses that make me look like a complete nerd. You can just imagine the bullies have a field day with me. I'm different, I'm clumsy, I'm ginger, I'm a speccy-four-eyes, I tend to count a lot, I look…

'DAI, I AM GOING TO COUNT. IF YOU ARE NOT IN THE KITCHEN IN 10 SECONDS NO WII FOR A WEEK. THAT'S ONE.'

…like a complete drip and…

'THAT'S TWO.'

...I don't listen to what anyone else says, or so I'm told.

'Coming Mum. Sorry!'

WIN

It's Friday. That means back to school, which is bad; Guillim is always worse on a Friday. Win thinks it's because he has to get some extra bullying in to carry him over the weekend, but I'm not so sure. I think it's more because there's football practice on Fridays and Win doesn't want to be reminded that we weren't picked for the team. At least it's double maths though, but I first have to navigate the minefield of breakfast.

This is always the hardest meal of the day, as there's no time to get it just right: just right means the right cereal in the correct bowl and not the red spoon - EVER. Toast, cut into two equal triangles, no butter just jam. Hot chocolate, that's not too hot and not too cold, served in the right mug. Goldilocks thought the three bears were fussy! The only one who ever comes near is Mum, but Mum on a good day when she's gotten out of bed on the right side and no one's asked her to do anything too strenuous first, like finding their car keys or ironing his shirt!

This is one of her good mornings, it's just a shame it doesn't turn out to be one of mine, but they say you can't have it all - at least breakfast was cool. Well, that is my Weetabix was: my hot chocolate was hot. Who's ever heard of cold hot chocolate?

Mum always drops me off at school on her way to work, which isn't quite so cool. Most of my frie...er...class-mates are allowed to make their own way, but they won't let me. Dad says I couldn't find my way out of a paper bag, let alone my way out of our Clos, something I'll remind him of in fifty years' time when he nags me to take him out of the old peoples home for a spin.

I think in their own way they're trying to look out for me. I've come home with one too many bruises and misplaced pieces of kit I haven't been able to think up a plausible enough excuse for, but making me more different is making it much worse.

Anyway, school is Oak Tree Junior, a square tall building coated in coffee and cream weather shield that stands all by itself on the corner of Creeper Avenue, which is just as well as the nearest landmark is the old decaying graveyard opposite. Whichever councillor thought of building a school opposite a whole pile of ancient crumbling tombstones either mustn't have had kids, or must have been having a laugh. This is the first place teachers look for erstwhile pupils having a sneaky fag at break times. It's gotten so bad the council has had to provide butt bins by the wrought iron gates.

I suppose it deters some of us, but for me I'd much rather spend my break amongst the dead than being hounded by the living. There's a lopsided gravestone belonging to 'The Greatly Missed William Roberts', or as we call him 'Billy Bob.' It's set back from the railings under the shade of a large oak tree that's the most comfortable to loll against while we eat our lunch. It has the added advantage of facing away from the entrance, which allows us to see without being seen. The amount of times my ol'e friend Billy Bob has saved me from a good thrashing is endless. It's almost as if I can feel him watching out and warning me when Guillim and his henchmen are on the warpath. Like that time last year when Win and my shoelaces became mysteriously knotted together ensuring we missed getting discovered by the terrible trio.

The school itself is surrounded by dark spiky railings to prevent sundry pupils from falling down the steep drop into the basement below. But this morning, for some reason, the railings seem different. A school tie and rucksack have mysteriously joined the rusty bicycle frame chained to the uppermost rust coloured spikes. My stomach lurches as I clock the rucksack; faded green denim I'd last seen slung over Win's left shoulder when he'd shouted, 'See yah later,' at the bottom of the school steps. I would recognise that bag anywhere with its frayed edges and large red ink stain on the front in the shape of Inner Mongolia. Grabbing my own bag, and without a second glance at my mum, I jump out of the car, slamming the door behind me.

Moments later I push open the finger smeared glass doors, frantically looking about for sign of Win.

Inside the school reception, I can smell the tension that seems to ooze, like sticky sweat, from the tatty cork notice boards lining the walls. I pause, albeit briefly, as I spot the Deputy Head, Four Chins Fothergill (Chemistry, Cookery and Elementary Chinese) poised, one foot on the lower rung of the steps, looking up at something that must have just disappeared out of sight around the top of the stairs.

Dropping my bags at his feet, I hurry past and fly up the staircase, ignoring his cries of, 'Where do you think you're going?' I can't rely on him for any help – he's not called Four Chins for nothing!

At the top of the stairs there's nothing to see. Classrooms on both sides, all with their doors closed, lockers at one end and not a student in sight. The last locker on the left catches my eye, Win's locker. Each child at Oak Tree Junior is issued with a locker on their first day that's just big enough for their bags and lunchbox - Win's padlock is broken, the door to his locker open and empty.

Before I can investigate, I hear shouts coming from Froggy's classroom (Miss Froggitt: ICT, English and Origami). I creep up to the door and peek through the crack in the door jam.

Greasy Guillim, unwashed hair matted to his skull has Win in a head lock, while his sidekicks Rob and Rory are holding a blue homework diary just out of reach.

'Rip it to pieces, Rob. It's only history, just like he'll be in five minutes, after I've finished with him.'

I just stand there, unable to move as the cold hand of fear trickles down my spine. It's never been this bad. Whilst they'd called us names and given us the odd slap and kick in passing, this level of intimidation was new, or was it? Maybe Win hadn't been telling me everything, and who could blame him?

What could a short little geek like me do to save the day? The bravest thing I've ever done was to…well actually I can't think of anything brave I've ever done. But that's not the point – Win's not perfect, but he doesn't deserve this, no one ever deserves to be bullied.

I scan the rest of the room even as I hope they won't notice my eye ball pressing up to the wood. I'm desperate, even though I know it's useless. I search for something, anything or anybody that can help, but there's no one about. The room is empty, apart from desks, chairs and a few books. There's nothing I can see to help. As I rack my brains, my eyes suddenly head towards the other end of the room and an idea pops into my head. I'm not sure how, or even if, it will work. However, as it's the only idea floating around in a cavern of emptiness, I have to give it a go.

Froggy's classroom is part of the IT suite and only separated from the computer section by a flimsy screen. I back away and make for this section, as quietly as I can. It only takes seconds for me to be standing in front of the work station we'd been using yesterday. Win and I'd been working on our DT project, which Mr Stringer (ICT, Map reading, Movies and Advanced Canoeing) had set us. But being us, we'd got distracted and had messed around with the microphones half way through the lesson. Turning up the volume to max, whilst silently thanking Froggy for always leaving the computers on standby, I press the play button and then hold my breath in hope. I'd no idea what was about to be played; we'd messed around with all sorts from Star War's to Dr Who and…oh no! I bury my head in my hands and squeeze my eyes shut. This could get ugly. Please, please, please don't let it be Papa Smurf.

'You've gotta ask yourself a question: Do you feel lucky? Well, do ya, punk?'

As I offer thanks to the force that is Clint Eastwood, I hear frantic footsteps running out of Froggy's room, followed by the sound of the door slamming into its frame with a resounding crash. I rush in to find Win lying on the floor, blood streaming from his nose and down onto his now strangely pink-stained shirt. Looking round, I notice bits of torn paper strewn all over the floor.

When he sees me tears start coursing down his cheeks, but not for long. He's learnt, as I have that crying doesn't get you anywhere: it only makes things worse. I turn away and head for the box of tissues on Froggy's table, feeling awkward. Despite Win being my best friend, I don't know how to comfort him. I know mum sometimes tries to put her arm around me when I'm distressed, but I just can't touch him. It makes me feel anxious just thinking about it.

I kneel on the floor and pick up bits of what look like last nights' homework, and in the awkward silence that follows, pick up the courage to ask him why Guillim has been beating him up.

'Oh the usual Dai - I'm not Welsh, I don't speak Welsh and I certainly don't look Welsh,' he mumbles. 'Apart from you, I have no friends and, by the looks of things, no future.'

I stare at him, not knowing what to say. I find it difficult to understand why anyone would bully boys as insignificant and unimportant as we are. But, whilst wanting to defend and support him, I know he's speaking the truth. Through no fault of his own his future looks bleak, even bleaker than mine. Win starts to dab the drip of blood hovering at the end of his nose and, looking at him properly, I notice for the first time his face as taken on a greyish tinge, not dissimilar to Mum's milk pudding.

'Win. I know what you're saying, but let's talk about this later and try to come up with a plan. For now, we need to get you patched up.' I stuff the rest of his homework into my pocket and escort him to the school nurses' office on the second floor.

Mrs Payne's sitting behind her desk, sorting through a pile of bandages left in disarray after yesterday's first aid lesson. But she takes one look at Win and, dropping the rest of them on the desk, heads to his side. However, she raises a finely plucked eyebrow when Win tells her he's just walked into the library door on his way to changing his reading book. With a sceptical look in my direction, she orders me back to class through pursed lips. I glance at Win over my shoulder, but he only manages a weak smile before the door closes behind me.

After going down to the caretakers' office on the ground floor, to report Win's abandoned rucksack, I run back upstairs to my classroom, sliding behind my battered wooden desk with only seconds to spare.

But I find I can't concentrate on anything as mundane as geography. My mind seems stuck on Win's words. I knew things weren't right, but I hadn't realised how bad it was. Guillim and his gang bullied everyone, including me. They'd always picked on me, but me being me meant that much of it washed over my head. Mostly I'm not aware of what people say about me, or for that matter what they say to me. I just know I have to stay away from them.

'Dai Monday! Are you actually awake? Can we expect your attention any time soon?'

The piercing voice of Mr Atoms (Science, Scrabble Club and Cross Stitch), interrupts my unhappy thoughts. Picking up my pencil that's fallen onto my notebook, I glance at the white board and try to look interested in fracking. There's no point in getting landed with extra homework for not paying attention. I'll ask Mum if I can visit Win later.

The Plan

After such an eventful morning, the afternoon crawls by. My main concern is to avoid Greasy Guillim and his crew. But they're all on the football team, and leave early to play in their last match of the season against Vickery High - it's the first time in three years I'm happy to be rubbish at football.

I'm allowed to catch the school bus home as it drops me off by the bus stop opposite our house. So at eleven minutes past four, I jump down the last step and lug my bags up our moss covered path, avoiding both the cracks and the slugs before dumping my kit just inside the back door.

'Is that you, Dai?' Mum shouts from upstairs. 'Its biscuits and milk for snack, they're on the table. I'll be down in a minute; I just have to sort out your dad's shoes before he comes home. Robin has thrown up in them again.'

All I want to do is nip next door to see Win, but I know Mum won't let me before homework, especially with having to clean up cat sick again!

I drain my milk and pull out my books. Half an hour later, with my homework sort of completed and stuffed into my book bag, I'm allowed to see if Win wants to play. I even have a plate of chocolate muffins to take with me. Only from the Deganwy Co-op, but he won't mind. He's been exposed to my mum's attempts at baking too many times in the past.

Buzz, his dad, opens the door at the second knock. He's very tall and very thin, with skin the colour of polished mahogany. His iron grey hair's cropped to his scalp, but that's not what most people remember. Mostly they remember his smile. Unlike most grown-ups I know, Buzz is in a good mood most of the time. It must be because of his cool job - even now his face breaks into a grin when he sees it's me.

'Can I see Win, please?' I ask, knowing his dad's strict on school nights. 'I won't stay long. Oh, and my mum gave me these for you,' I add, holding out the plate.

'Of course you can, he'll be pleased to see you after that accident in the library,' Buzz replies.

I look up, but there's no trace of suspicion, or disbelief on his face. His voice follows me as I walk up the stairs. 'And don't forget to thank your mum for the cakes.'

'Will do.'

Win's door's open, but I knock anyway, before walking into his room. He's lying across his bed watching TV, his face glued to the little screen in front of him. I glance around his room, which is as familiar to me as mine, familiar but very different. For a start, his is twice the size of mine, with a sloping roof and large dormer windows with blue curtains. His dad painted the walls blue too (his favourite colour), and put up white MDF shelves for all his books; Win loved to read. Books, comics, magazines, leaflets - you name it, Win reads it. He's particularly interested in history, although I have no idea why.

There's also a plain white wardrobe next to the fireplace and a second-hand desk with a blue swivel chair. I head for the large comfy chair in the corner.

'Hey Win, what you watching?' I ask, glancing towards the TV.

'A rerun of Dad's Army,' he mutters, eyes still glued to the screen. So I join him in silence for the last ten minutes of Pike being called 'Stupid boy.'

The music fades out and I suddenly wish I'm anywhere but sitting next to my best friend and having nothing to say. As I'm sure you've gathered, I'm rubbish at any form of communication, unless there's a games console involved. I've been straining my brain for hours as to how I could make Win feel better, and I'd come up with nothing useful, except an idea that might buy me more thinking time.

I watch him reach out to pick up the remote, and pluck up the courage to ask him what he's up to after football practice tomorrow.

'Mum has to work as it's the end of year inventory. If you haven't anything better to do, I thought we could have another look at the towers? I'm sure she'll let us.'

His face lights up like a light bulb – it's the first time in ages I've actually done something right.

Win loves history, and my mum works at Conwy Castle, which is steeped in history from the top of its 13th Century towers to the bottom of its creepy dungeons. It also has the added attraction of more than its fair share of ghosts, with one in each turret and a few others as spares. She's always coming home with new tales of scared tourists being chased by spooky spooks.

But then his grin vanishes back inside his face.

'Are you sure your mum won't mind? Remember what happened last time?'

'Ah yesss, but that was different,' I say, with more confidence than I feet. 'Having a tummy bug can happen to anyone…'

Even then, it wouldn't have been so bad if we hadn't visited the gift shop first. I really don't know what Gwyneth and Dilys were thinking, throwing up into their carrier bags. They should have known they were only made from recycled paper – what a stink! Mum said it took ages to get rid of the smell of vomit from the Great Hall.

He looks back at me, a giggly grin spreading across his face, and suddenly we're both in fits of laughter. Gwyneth and Dilys, the darlings of Year Six, screaming as the bags split at the seams and vomit dripped down their grey tights and onto their shiny new patent school shoes. That was the best day ever. The only thing that could have topped it was if Guillim had joined the puke party. But he just watched, whilst taking photos on his phone - no doubt for some harassment campaign later.

Why is it that bullies always come off best? My dad is always saying *'What goes around comes around,'* but what does he know? Everyone is scared of Guillim - me, Win, the whole of Year Six and all of the teachers – EVERYONE and it's just my luck he lives on our clos!

Win and I reminisce for another seven and three-quarter minutes before making arrangements to meet at eleven o'clock the next morning. We live in the road but one next to the Castle. Sammy can even see three turrets from her bedroom window, which is such a waste. Even if she was interested in the view, she's visually disadvantaged with layer upon layer of mascara gluing her eyes open in what we call the matt cat look!

The next day is Saturday. Saturdays are always less frantic than week-days, or they usually are. But, this Saturday Mum left early and Dad gave me the red spoon.

I'm not even going to go there. I've more important stuff to tell you. But he really should have known better. He HAS lived with me for ten years, three months and fourteen days now. He was rushing, as usual, but today was different as he was taking Sammy to play netball in Manchester and he didn't want to miss his train. At least he was cool about us visiting Mum at the Castle instead of making us stay with Win's dad.

After returning from an uneventful football practice, I race upstairs to pack my rucksack with my notebook and pen that I never leave the house without. Some boys (well most of the boys at my school) collect football cards, but not me. I collect numbers, but not any old numbers, special palindrome ones.

I have always collected them, ever since I can remember. It's the same with words, like Radar and Kayak that can be read backwards or forwards, but I prefer number ones. My favourite one is our postman, Davey Lloyd's birthday; 29.2.92. There aren't many five year old posties employed by the Post Office. I always remember to wish him a Happy Birthday; it's only every four years after all! I bet he's well hacked off at only getting birthday presents every Leap Year, I would be.

Win's waiting for me at the end of the garden, and we walk through the green wrought iron gate into the lane. This pigeon poo and dog turd splattered path is the quickest way to the Castle entrance - no wonder Mum is always on about me removing my shoes in the hall.

The sky is a clear blue without a cloud in sight, although this doesn't stop us from wearing our anoraks, more out of habit than anything. This is Wales we're talking about, where it seems to rain just for fun pretty much all year round.

It just takes us six minutes to arrive at the entrance, but we should have walked faster as a bus load of assorted camera-slinging, back-packing tourists pushes in front of us to the ticket desk. Luckily it's the familiar florid-faced Mr Everude-Williams that's manning the counter today – he's sure to help as he's known me ever since I grew out of pull-ups. When he spots us trying, and failing, to squeeze from behind the bottom of a woman in a purple baseball cap, he raises his hand allowing us to queue jump past her and her disgruntled bus party. To shouts of 'Hey you, get back in line,' we round the corner into the Visitor Centre.

Mum's at one end in the gifts section. She's balancing precariously on the top rung of a rickety wooden ladder, arranging what looks like large lumps of pottery on the top shelf. She mutters her standard warning about being careful on the walkways before turning her attention back to an ugly red vase in the shape of a bunch of grapes.

'Where to first, Win?' Although I don't need to ask. Win has always been more interested in the *Chapel Tower* than anywhere. It's here where most of the strange happenings occur, from lingering smells of incense to actual ghost sightings. The most recent sighting made the newspapers only last week.

Apparently thirteen year old twins, Reya and Freddy Bakernut, had visited the Castle with their parents to help with their school project on Edward the First. They'd separated on arrival, as Reya was desperate for a wee and Freddy wouldn't wait. But, when they met back in the inner courtyard, they were both as white as sheets. Reya started to describe seeing a hazy apparition dressed in armour, but Freddy interrupted, completing the description by adding thick black boots and a long ornate sword. They'd both seen the same ghost, even though Reya had been by the well and Freddy was standing in the middle of the *Chapel Tower*!

'To the *Chapel Tower*,' Win shouts.

We make our way along the wooden bridge and across the courtyard to the stone steps. All is quiet as we're the first to head this way, which is just the way we like it. No one to annoy us, or keep an eye on what we're up to, even when it's not much.

We'd climbed up fifteen out of the thirty, shallow, well-worn steps of the spiral staircase that would take us to the upper chamber of the tower when Win suddenly stops without warning, causing me to careen into his back.

He glances at me over his shoulder. 'What's that smell?'

'Well it's not me, and for goodness sake look where you're going in future,' I retort, checking my elbow that's banged against the wall during 'the pile up.'

But I can sort of smell something as well - something sickly sweet, a bit like that air freshener mum got cheap down the market. The one Dad mistook for antiperspirant, and ended up being attacked by a swarm of flies as soon as he'd walked out of the front door. Mum laughed herself silly for weeks.

The smell was getting stronger now. I look around to find the source, only to spot a grey mist oozing up from the cracks in the floor ahead of us.

'I don't think we should go in, maybe it's a fire,' I squeak, but Win doesn't hear me. I watch him move away and walk towards the mist, his eyes fixed on the wall in front of him.

I follow, making sure that I don't walk on any of the cracks between the paving slabs. I don't like this and I don't want to be here, so I concentrate on the slabs underneath my feet instead. I'll do anything to avoid the current situation, to avoid looking at the mist as it seems to shift and shape into the outline of a person, but it's too late. All's silent, except for the hammer of my heart as it thumps like an exploding cannonball underneath my anorak.

I squint behind my glasses in order to get a better look and suddenly there in front of us is the figure of a man, where seconds before there'd been only mist. A short bent figure, older than old and wearing tarnished armour partially covered by a faded red cloak. He's in the process of unsheathing an engraved sword from a scabbard strapped to his left hip. But it's his red-rimmed bloodshot eyes glaring at me that scare me more than anything.

I draw up beside Win with the intention of pulling him away, but one look into those ancient all-knowing eyes and I'm transfixed. My feet take root as if someone's just filled my trainers with quick-setting cement. All I can do is stand and stare at this vision, as all around the temperature in the tower plummets to sub-zero. As I stare, I see his dry, cracked lips starting to move and then form words.

'Where is my crown?' it says in a voice that sends shivers down my spine. 'Britain will never be great if you do not return my crown. This is not enough to secure your future. Only what seems impossible will be possible.'

Win turns to look at me, his eyebrows raised as if to say. *'Do you know what he's talking about?'*

How on earth would I know? Honestly! I thought that he'd at least have been able to work that one out. Now if he'd asked how many Try's Wales had scored in the last ten years that would have been different, but crowns and the like – not a hope! Anyway he's the history nut, not me. I shake my head and watch him turn back.

'What crown?'

But the words get lost in a sudden noise that fills the room, not dissimilar to a herd of elephants trampling up the stairs. With one last look from those dreadful eyes the ghost in front of us starts to fade and disappear. When, seven seconds later, the purple hatted woman and her companions enter the chapel, only the last vestige of mist remains, curling around the bottom of the wall as it floats through the cracks. As it disappears, I notice just a few water droplets glistening in the dim sunlight streaming through the small arrow slits that slash the walls.

We're suddenly surrounded by a shedload of tourists. The crescendo of voices cut through the silence like my dad's lawnmower cutting grass. I have to get away. It's too crowded, and I'm about to get squashed again by Mrs Purple Hat's hammer-throwing thighs. I yell at Win that I'll see him downstairs and squeeze myself to the door, trying not to touch anyone on my way.

'One, two, three, four. Breathe. Five, six, seven. Only twenty three steps to go. Eight, nine...'

Twenty one steps and two minutes later, my heart has stopped thumping against my ribs. I still feel...what? Weak: yes. Scared: certainly. But mainly confused and fed up. All I want is a quiet life with no excitement, and what do I get when I try and do a favour for a pal? A mad-eyed ghost on a mission.

Win sits down on the bottom step beside me.

'Dai, wasn't that the coolest ever? Did you see his eyes? And what do you think that was about with the crown and all?' he whispers, wrapping his arms around him to try and get warm, just like I'd done only seconds before. At least the weak Welsh sun peeking through the clouds offered some warmth. The Tower had been so cold, too cold.

I look at him in absolute horror. I'd never seen him so excited over anything, even when he'd won the history prize in Year Five with a score of ninety seven percent. An excited Win was just as difficult to cope with as a persecuted one. I just knew I was going to be dragged out of my comfort zone, and into a much scarier one.

'You're bonkers. Did you actually see how sharp that sword was?' I said, knowing all too well that it wouldn't get me anywhere - he was too far gone for that.

'Come on, Dai. This is the most exciting thing that's happened in Conwy since Mr Parry fished out poor old Mrs Lewis's false teeth from the estuary after that seagull stole her battered cod mid-bite. We can't ignore what we've just seen, and I for one am going to try to find out what the ghost was on about. Are you with me, or not?'

Looking at Win, what choice do I have? Help him, or lose my best friend, my only friend, perhaps forever. It's easy to share sweets when you've a boxful - but when you have only one, and little chance of being given any more, well that's a different choice altogether.

It would have been a much easier decision if I'd known the choice I was about to make would change everything. After today, things would never be the same. But that's tomorrow and I still have to answer Win.

'Oh I suppose so,' I mumble, before adding with a final flare of bravado, 'I'll help you investigate, but at the first sign of danger, I'm off.'

Behind us, the noise of feet pounding down the stone steps reverberates around the walls. We make our way towards the cellar and out into the castle gardens.

Arty

We wander about the outer ward in a bit of a daze – it's all an anti-climax. How can wandering around ruins ever beat meeting an ancient ruin in person? And what was all that about crowns anyway? I try to remember his exact words. He'd said something about returning Britain's crown or something? I glance over at the slumped shoulders of my best friend, and note with some satisfaction that at least he looks as confused as me. How on earth are two ten year olds meant to figure it all out, and why did he pick on us anyway? I thought back to the other ghost sightings Mum had mentioned over the years and remember quite a few had involved children. There has to be a reason, but I can't for the life of me think of one.

All this thinking of ghost sightings reminds me that Mum keeps a record of everything that goes on at the castle, including ghost sightings. As manager of the gift shop, she's in the unique position of being able to pick up all the tit bits of gossip as visitors walk through on the way to the exit. She collected everything in a large black file, along with any newspaper cuttings. She was always saying that when she retired she was going to write a book and make her fortune – yeah right!

I drag a surprised Win back towards the entrance and find her on ground level, pricing up some odd shaped mugs.

'What are you doing back so soon?' She picks up a grey cup in the shape of a lopsided penguin. 'You haven't been getting into any trouble, have you?'

'No way, Mum. We were just discussing the ghost sighting you've been telling me about – do you still have that file?' I say, not wanting her to know how interested we are. Perhaps we'd at least find some clues to his identity.

'Yes, dear, and you can borrow it for half an hour if you promise to return it safe and sound.' She reaches under the counter to pull out a dusty old folder.

'Now boys,' she looks us both in the eye. 'You have to be very careful with this; it takes me ages to keep it up to date.'

'Okay, you can trust me. We'll only take it to the bench outside.' I pick up the file, placing it under my arm.

As I turn to speak to Win, I find myself bumping into that purple-hatted woman again. She's alone this time and standing just behind the door browsing through the postcard rack. Maybe she's not with the other tourists after all, although it's a bit strange that she seems to be everywhere we happen to be. I give her a second glance, noticing the bulging flanks tapering to ridiculously small feet encased in black high heel boots, similar to a pair that Mum doesn't know Sammy owns. As I look upwards, all I can make out under the hat is a moon round face with bright pink cheeks and little black piggy eyes. Any minute now and she'll start to oink.

Once outside, I dump my rucksack on the ground and rummage for my notebook: if Win is serious about this I might as well make some notes, starting with trying to remember the ghost's exact words. After five minutes and three scribbled out pages we end up with,

Where is my crown? Britain will not be great without it. The impossible will be possible.

It's not exact, but that's the best that we can do under the circumstances.

Next comes mum's file, which reminds me a little of our house - stuffed to the brim with all and sundry with no signs of organisation, although I blush slightly remembering my empty sock drawer.

After thirty minutes of careful reading, we discover there are forty nine articles about the Castle, dating back to when mum started working at the centre. I thought it would have been much more. However, there are only three that could be our man.

'Look Dai, here's the story from last week we were talking about,' said Win, his finger jabbing at the last article in the folder. We both reread it from start to finish, eager to discover anything new about our ghost, but Win had remembered it all exactly as it had been written.

Nevertheless, I jot down the children's names and the date of the sighting on a new page headed:

Dai and Win Investigate

The other two sightings were also by children, which is a little unusual – it crosses my mind that they could have made them up, but I read them anyway.

The first happened two years ago, on the eleventh of December when Gracie Gardiner, then aged nine, was visiting from Llandudno with her Granny Ann. She was in the Watching Chamber, spying through the peephole down at the chapel, when she spotted what she thought was a soldier crawling along the floor by the window, as if he'd dropped something. However, when her gran looked up, the Chapel was empty. It sounded all a bit suspect, but I add Gracie's name, address and date to my list.

The last entry isn't as exciting as the other two and very suspicious. For a start, the girl is only four-years-old. I wouldn't have included it except that she'd reported it to Mum and who am I to argue with my mum?

Emily was visiting the *Chapel Tower* with her parents and younger brother, Jack. As soon as she'd walked into the tower she'd felt someone touch her hand and whisper, 'I am Arty Dragon, I command thee to help me.'

She was adamant these were his exact words and she wouldn't leave the Castle until her parents had told Mum about it. It was all very peculiar; however it didn't stop me from adding the newspaper date along with the girl's details to the bottom of my list.

Win and I stare at the short list, both none the wiser.

Reya and Freddy Bakernut from Conwy (newspaper dated the thirteenth of December). Ghost searching for treasure.

Gracie Gardiner from Llandudno. Date ghost seen on the eleventh of December. Ghost searching wall in *Chapel Tower*.

Emily Frost, no address, (newspaper date the fifteenth of December). Ghost called Arty Dragon.

'Now isn't that funny? All the sightings occur on, or around the eleventh of December.' Win strokes his chin.

He's right, of course and I feel a bit cross that he's spotted it first.

'Yesss.' I pause, giving my brain enough time to think up a clever reply. 'Or that they all occurred on the eleventh, and it took Mum a few days to write them down?' I point to the open folder, full to the brim of tatty bits of paper. 'It's not as if my mum's known for her filing system, now is it?'

Win looks non-committal, but I'll show him.

'How do you fancy a trip to the library, so we can check the dates? I don't think Mum will mind, I'll ask her when I drop off the folder.' I say, slamming my notebook shut and placing it in my rucksack. We both head back towards the gift shop in silent agreement.

There is no further sign of the purple-hatted woman - she's probably gone off to find the nearest pigsty for a rest, along with the rest of the bus party.

Half an hour later finds us installed in one of the work stations at the library. The library is, luckily enough, just down the road from the castle or, as sure as chocolate buttons melt Mum wouldn't have let us go. But this time she just waves us away with a wave of her hand and a fiver, with strict instructions to buy a pie from Roberts for our lunch.

Win sits in front of the keyboard, his facial features set in concentration and anticipation. After a minute of trying to locate the Google icon, hidden among all the others, he types, 'Eleventh December, Conwy' in the search bar.

We weren't expecting to find anything, that would have been too easy, but why does it have to be this difficult?

He starts to read from the first hit, stumbling over the words, which isn't really surprising.

'Llywelyn ap Gruffudd, the last Welsh Prince of Wales, died on the eleventh of December, 1282.'

Even with Win's ninety seven percent history success, he hasn't a clue who that is, and there's no good asking me, I'd only scraped by with a meagre fifty one.

I see the misery in his face. 'I know I'm useless at typing, but can I have a quick go?'

He shrugs, before shifting up and pushing the mouse in my direction. I blink at the screen and then, with one finger type in Llywelyn ap Gruffudd (as names go this is even worse than my one) into the Google text box, followed by the word 'crown,' and then wait, fingers hovering over the keys.

I never thought that we would find anything useful. Win and I aren't destined to set the world alight. We're destined to just drift, from one disaster to another in the hope of coming through the other side unscathed. But just for once I'm wrong! I look at Win as he glances down at all the hits, not for Llewellyn's crown - but for the crown of Arthur Pendragon.

'Win.' I squeak, not daring to believe the screen. 'Do you think Emily-what's-her-face meant to say Arthur Pendragon, instead of Arty Dragon?'

'No way, that's impossible, isn't it?' his voice trailing off into a scarcely audible whisper.

I scroll down the page, looking for any other interesting snippets of information.

'Look at this site.' I point to the paragraph in front of us. 'It says that King Edward took the 'Coron Arthur' off the then Prince of Wales, Llywelyn ap Gruffudd, after his capture in 1282, but that the crown used to belong to King Arthur of the round table.'

We stare at each other in silence, my thoughts clearly reflected on his face. Win Bee and Dai Monday, the most unlikely partnership since prawn cocktail crisps, have been sent on a quest to find King Arthur's crown. How mad is that? And I didn't even know he had a crown, only a sword in the stone thingy.

Hold on a minute though, it doesn't make any sense. I stare at the hundreds of entries on the screen without seeing any of them, thinking back over everything I know about King Arthur. True, it doesn't amount to much, but I do know he never existed. He was a sort of fairy-tale figure, wasn't he? I turn in my seat to face Win.

'Are you thinking what I'm thinking? I thought *King Arthur and the Knights of the Round Table* was a story. What about that series we watched on the telly? You know, the one where Merlin had the funny eyes?'

'I don't know what to make of it all. First ghosts and now King Arthur. If I didn't know any better, Dai, I'd think that Guillim was involved. I fully expect him to jump out from behind those shelves over there,' he adds, lifting up his hand.

But that doesn't stop me from glancing over my shoulder in the direction he's pointing.

'Well, this is a library, why don't we see if there are any books?'

I wander over to the desk to ask the slim girl with the frizzy ponytail for some on King Arthur. She gives me a funny look before pointing me in the right direction. There are only six but that isn't a problem in itself, except I don't know which one to pick. In the end I just choose one at random and head back to the work station.

The book's entitled 'King Arthur, Knight by night and day' by Cecelia A Moon. The story of King Arthur, for five to seven-year-olds; Well at least we should be able to understand it.

'Once upon a time there was a great king, Uther Pendragon. On his death the great wizard Merlin drove a mighty sword into a stone. The person to first pull the sword from the stone would be the next king. Many knights tried but a lowly groom, Arthur, ended up removing the sword and therefore became King - King Arthur. Arthur carried two swords with him. The sword from the stone and Excalibur, presented to him by the lady in the lake.

Arthur had to fight many battles to secure his throne but, after many years, he built his castle, Camelot, and married a beautiful maiden called Guinevere. For many years he lived in peace with his knights of the round table, until he was betrayed by his bravest knight, Lancelot. During his last battle in pursuit of the Holy Grail, Arthur was fatally wounded by his son Mordred and carried off to the Isle of Avalon.

Galahad, Lancelot's son, found the Grail as he was the purest of them all.'

We don't know what to make of it, it sounded very much like a fairy-tale, with little facts to speak of. However that doesn't stop me from turning to a new page of my notebook and adding the following:

Current facts
Ghost seen by Win and me and three others on, or around the eleventh of December, trying to find treasure, maybe crown.
Ghost maybe that of Arthur Pendragon.
11th December 1282 date of L.A. Gruffudd's death.
After his death King Edward took the crown and it hasn't been seen since.

How could both Win and me have seen King Arthur's ghost if he'd never existed?
Feeling both disillusioned and confused Win and I decide to call it a day and start to make our way back home, via Roberts for some sausage rolls. It's already past lunchtime and Win still has all his homework to do, while I have a mystery to puzzle over.

The Break-in

Much later, when climbing into bed, I think about the rest of the day. It had been pretty nondescript and had ended with the usual slouching in front of the TV with a Chinese.

I tuck my Star Wars duvet around my neck to keep the drafts out, all the while wishing that I could keep thoughts of Arthur at bay just as easily. Pictures of dragons and pointy-hatted damsels in distress swirl around my head and even thoughts of the odd sheep won't dislodge them. At least all this excitement seems to have distracted Win; he hasn't mentioned Greasy Guillim or his crew even once.

I must have dropped off to sleep because the next thing I know, someone is shaking my shoulder.

'Dai, Dai wake up.'

'What, what is it? What do you want?' I start to wrestle with my tangled duvet, my eyes refusing to open against the glare of the light-filled room. 'What time is it?'

'It's only three o'clock, but I've had a call,' says mum, yanking the duvet off me. 'There's been a break-in at the castle, and I have to meet the police to see if anything's been taken. I'm really sorry, Dai, but with your dad and sister both away, you'll have to come with me. Dress up warm in your blue fleece and don't forget your hat and gloves – it's going to be cold at this time of the morning.'

I just look at her, clutching the edges of her white and black Dalmatian dressing gown together, her reddish brown hair standing on end. A break-in at the castle, why? Who would want to burgle the castle? There certainly wasn't anything of value, unless of course she meant the gift shop. I glance at her and she manages to hold my eye – not an easy thing to do where I'm concerned

'Dai, stop thinking and hurry up, would you, just for once please? I'll see you downstairs in five minutes.' She hurries out of the room - hopefully to comb her hair.

I groan, but follow orders, remembering just in time to stuff my notepad into my rucksack. It's going to be a long night, or should that be a long morning?

When we arrive at the castle we find it in complete darkness – most unusual as it's always lit up like a Christmas tree whatever the time of year. At the main door I see a crowbar heading my way, but thankfully this one's covered in plastic and being carried to one of the police cars. And then I notice the grass, shining like diamonds in the pale light cast my mum's torch. But they aren't diamonds; they're shards of glass that crunch under the thin soles of my trainers, even as I try to avoid them.

I grab at Mum's hand and feel her curl her fingers around mine. It's not because I'm scared, well I am a little bit, it's because I can see she's upset. Nothing like this has ever happened to us before.

A short, black-haired, square policeman, not much taller than Sammy, accosts us as we walk into the centre. Mum explains who she is and who I am but he just stands and stares at me, with a big question mark scrawled across his face. In fact, if he raises his eyebrows anymore they'll disappear under his helmet.

It takes Mum ten minutes to check the centre - but it's all very strange as nothing appears to be missing. The till hasn't been touched and the Ugly Mugs, obviously very valuable in all their hideousness, are lined up as usual. In fact, the only thing that's been touched is the folder on ghost sightings. Or, to be exact, the folder is there, but all the contents have been removed. I almost fall off my chair in amazement. Why would anyone take a list of ghost sightings, unless it has something to do with our ghost?

'It's peculiar, Dai. Not many people know that I collect this, only the staff at the centre, come to think of it.' She pauses. 'Although there was a lady yesterday…'

'Did she have a purple hat on?' I ask, without thinking.

'How do you know that?' It's Mum's turn to look shocked. But before I can answer, the black-haired DCI has joined us to ask if there's anything of value in the *chapel tower*. My head shoots up, as if he'd just mentioned the Wales England cup final.

'The door to the tower's been jemmied open. It does look as if it may have been vandals, after all. They've caused quite a lot of damage up there.'

She follows him out of the centre, heading towards the castle and I trail after them both.

'Alright and where do you think you're going?' booms a voice behind me.

'Mum, can I come along, pleeasse?' I plead. 'I won't touch anything and I was up at the Chapel yesterday, so I might be able to see something.'

Mum looks at me for what feels like forever. She knows I'm up to something, but not what, and I'm not about to tell her anything in front of anyone with eyebrows like that.

'I think that would be a good idea.' I watch as she turns to face the DCI to give him one of her special smiles. The one she normally reserves for Dad when she wants him to assemble anything flat pack. 'He may be able to help. He's always messing about in the towers, and he is quite observant. I'll make sure he doesn't interfere with anything.'

But to me she whispers, 'What are you up to? I hope you haven't got yourself messed up in anything.' Grabbing my hand, we follow the policeman out of the centre and towards the tower.

The damage is clear to see. The door's splintered, the wood chipped where presumably the same crow bar has been used to jemmy it open. It's even worse when we enter the Chapel itself. Someone has used some sort of tool to gouge the mortar from between the bricks under the window. The bricks are now scarred with deep slashes, as if someone had been very angry at the time. Poor Mum, I can feel her shaking through my gloved hand, but if she squeezes any harder I won't be able to pick my nose for a week.

'Who would do this?' she says, her voice almost a whisper. 'What's the point of damaging the wall just here? I just don't understand any of it.' She turns away and heads for the doorway.

I look at her and then at the wall. Without realising the significance of what she'd said, she's hit the nail on the head. The wall has been damaged close to where the ghost had stood. He'd been standing about thirty centimetres to the left of the damage. He'd been standing too far away for the damage to be of any significance. He'd been standing…My eyes snag onto a small hole in the wall far above our heads and I slap my hand to my head in frustration. Of course, how stupid! He'd been standing in the exact same place when Gracie-what's-her-name had spied him through the *Watching Room*. I make my way up to Mr Eyebrows. I just have to get into the *Watching Room* and I'll do whatever it takes, including being polite.

'Excuse me, sir; has anyone checked the *Watching Room* that leads off this?'

He glances at me as if I've just crawled out from under a stone, his eyebrows heading north again. But good old Mum jumps at my suggestion.

'That's right. Good idea, why didn't I think of it? There may be damage up there too, although I hope not. Why don't you show the officer how to get to it - if that's okay with you, that is?'

He looks at me, his mouth set in a thin line of disapproval. With a quick nod of his head he waves me forward before following me out and up the well-worn stone steps.

The *Watching Room* is untouched, but I didn't expect it to be otherwise. I needed to get up here to see through the eyes of that little girl. I just know that this isn't the work of random mindless vandals. Somebody is looking for something that's linked to our ghost, and I'm pretty sure they'd looked in the right place. But exactly what they were looking for was anybody's guess.

When we reach the chamber, I try to show him the king's spying hole, but he's not interested. He turns abruptly, indicating with his hand that I should follow and its then I take my chance to steal a look through the gap in the wall. In that split second, I see the angle Gracie saw her ghost. It's as I thought - too far left from where the bricks had been damaged.

I need to take a closer look, but how on earth am I going to do that without the police, or Mum becoming suspicious? Mum could already read me and Win like a book. She never lets me get away with anything.

"Well, we're about done here, until the dusting team have finished that is. You might as well go home, Mrs. Monday and try and get some sleep. Please don't speak to anyone until we know more about what's actually happened.' He gives me another shaggy brow glare, before turning on his heels with a military click. Who did he think he was, the SAS or something?

I don't remember much of the walk home, except it was even colder than before. My teeth chattered away to themselves quite happily, with no interference from me. Mind you, I wouldn't have been able to add anything useful to the conversation anyway. My brain felt as numb as my body. In fact, I was pretty sure that I'd left my feet back at the castle – I haven't been able to feel them for a good five minutes.

The inky black night is alight with stars spangled across its darkness, for once visible in a cloudless sky. But I'm far too tired to give it more than a cursory glance. It's only then that I realise just what an ordeal it's been. I glance at my watch, just visible in the moonlight – It's already half past four.

Despite being wrapped up like a Beef Wellington, I'm overcome with tiredness not to mention chilled to the bone.

'Dai, straight up to bed, we'll talk tomorrow,' Mum says, a gentle warning in her voice. 'You've been good tonight.' At least she didn't tack 'for once' on like she usually does.

Police

The next thing I know, shafts of pale sunlight are streaming through the crack between my Star Wars curtains, and the smell of bacon frying is wafting upstairs. I jump out of bed but my body aches as if it's been wrung out like a flannel.

Mum's waiting for me at the kitchen table, cradling her cup of tea between interlaced fingers. However she lets me eat my bacon sandwich in peace, before the interrogation begins in earnest. A cooked breakfast is a rarity in our house, but as a way of softening me up, it works a treat. Before even the last crispy bit of rind is swallowed, I've already started to spill the beans about the Purple Lady and the ghost sightings. I have to tell her about the ghost that Win and I'd seen but, by her expression I think that she'd already guessed. She is more interested in the Purple Lady, and all I can tell her is that I'd spotted her at the castle ticket office.

'What did she look like?' she asks, adding more sugar to her cup. 'I remember that she asked about ghost sightings, but I was still trying to sort out that new order of pottery, so I wasn't paying attention.'

That's another thing about parents that really bugs me. They live with you for ten years and they still don't remember the most basic things about you. If I can't remember my football kit on Mondays, my PE kit on Tuesdays, my swim kit on Wednesdays or that leaving my clothes where they land makes aforesaid parents go ballistic, I'm certainly not going to remember what someone that I only saw for like three minutes looked like.

'All I can remember is that she had a big bottom, as I had to squeeze past it at the ticket desk and that she reminded me of a pig. I couldn't see her hair, it was hidden under her hat and the brim was down, so I didn't notice her face.'

'It sounds as if she was in disguise, doesn't it?' she says, and now that I think about it she's probably right.

'Perhaps Win will remember more, I'm seeing him out back later.' I glance up, barely noticing her pale, tired face. My brain is more interested in working out how to get a closer look at that wall.

'Do you have to go back to the castle later then?'

'Dai Monday, what are you up to?' she snaps. 'You never want to come to the castle. After yesterday I was going to ask Mr Bee to look after you.'

'But but…..' I stumble, trying to think of a way to get around her. 'You're always nagging me to spend less time on electronic games, and this castle business is fascinating. I promise I won't be in the way, I just want to help, and I may remember more about the Purple Lady.'

'I'll only let you come with me if you promise to behave.'

I look at her uncertain expression and know I've won. Being different has one or two advantages. For some strange reason, baby-sitters won't sit with me, not since that last time when I spent the whole evening reciting the times tables at the girl down the road. I got right up to 2400 x 12 (the answer's 28800, but you probably know that, right)?

Later, when I see Win outside, he's pig sick when he hears about the break in.

'That's not fair. I saw him first and yet you get all the fun.'

'Yeah, right! If you can call it fun, being dragged out of bed in the middle of the night,' I yell back.

After he's calmed down a bit I go on to tell him about the damage to the chapel wall. He's as puzzled as I am but, at least he agrees there must be something hidden. What, is the question?

'Do you remember any more about the Purple Lady? Mum's nagging me, and you know what I'm like.'

'Don't you remember how short she was, as well as round – a bit like a beach ball, but a beach ball wearing thick black glasses?'

'Of course, now why didn't I remember that?' At least I had something to tell Mum and that DCI, if he was there.

He's there and looking none too pleased to see me, until Mum explains there is nobody she can leave me with, and that I'm still too young to be left alone. He drags her off into a corner and starts whispering in muffled tones, but I can still make out the odd word.

'Prints, no match, tower cleaned, purple hat.' I decide to make my way to the tower as the finger printers must have finished by now.

This time there's no one to stop me, even though I've an excuse all lined up just in case - I'd made sure to leave my favourite parker pen in the tower, the one that Granny Gosh had given me for my birthday, I just hope it's a good enough excuse if I'm spotted.

I head straight to the place I'm certain our ghost appeared. Kneeling down, and feeling the cold hard floor dig into my skin I examine each of the bricks, looking for imperfections, cracks or anything unusual. To be honest, I don't know what I'm meant to be looking for. I start from the bottom and, working from left to right inspect a span of six bricks across. The bricks are stained with age, but all seem to be the same shade of muddy grey and yellow. Each brick is separated from the next by old mortar, the colour of damp sand that crumbles to the touch.

I'm about to give up when I spot something. On the third row there's a small hole in the mortar, about the size of a penny. I wish I'd brought my ruler, as I'd be able to tell you how many millimetres it is. Even then, I wouldn't have bothered with it except that it's a concentric circle within a well preserved section of mortar with otherwise little signs of wear and tear.

Why?

I grab my pen from the floor where I'd placed it earlier and start to unscrew the barrel, revealing the thin metal cartridge. Stuffing the remaining pieces in my pocket, I poke the end of the cartridge into the hole in order to remove some of the mortar, but as I lever the end towards me I can see what looks like the end of little tube peeking out of the hole. I continue wriggling the cartridge backwards and forwards until I'm able to grab the end between my thumb and forefinger. As I ease the tube out, it's followed by dust and mortar particles that form a little mound on the floor below.

I must have been concentrating so hard I didn't hear the noises from downstairs until they're just outside the door. I move away from the wall, slipping the tube up my sleeve even as I hear a voice say, 'who told you that you could come up here?'

It's old eyebrows again and he doesn't look happy. Doesn't he have anything better to do than to follow me?

'Er, sorry about that, sir,' I say in my most innocent voice. 'I lost my pen up here yesterday so I thought I'd try and find it.' I reach into my pocket and pull out the pieces. 'It must have come apart when I dropped it; I hope I can put it together again. It was a present from my gran.'

I make my way to the doorway, hoping against hope that he won't spot the new pile of dust on the floor. In fact, the only pile of dust since the rest has been cleared up.

It takes a few minutes for Mum to finish with the police, while I hop from one foot to the next, gripping the cuff of my fleece to try and stop whatever it is shooting out the end of my sleeve - that would be a disaster. I'm able to drag her home, but only after she's phoned all the staff so that the castle can reopen later.

As we walk the short distance to our clos I have the strangest feeling that we aren't alone. Conwy isn't the centre of the Universe by any means and on a Sunday morning there's more life in the local graveyard than there is on our streets. All the same, I find myself glancing over my shoulder to see if we are being followed, which is stupid – who would want to follow us? Even so, I only start to relax when Mum's key turns in the lock.

As soon as we arrive home I ditch my coat and shoes, before heading to find her. She's in the kitchen, reaching in the back of the cupboard behind the washing-up-liquid for the emergency packet of chocolate digestives. Sammy and I think it's the coolest place ever – Dad's been searching for months...

'I've finished all my homework. Do you mind if I invite Win around to play on the Wii?' This is something that happens most weekends, so I know she'll agree.

'That's fine, but only until midday.' She looks up with bulging cheeks. 'Don't forget we've got to pick your sister up from the train station.'

Ten minutes later, with the lounge door shut and Mum still happily holed up in the kitchen, doing what Mums' do, I let the tube slide down my sleeve and land into my open palm, just like a magician. I know I'm showing off, but if you can't show off a little in front of your best friend, it's a bad job.

A long, tightly rolled piece of old parchment lay in the middle of my hand. I set it down on our dining table and start to unroll what turns out to be a very old letter. The writing is all faded grey loops and difficult to read, apart from the signature scrawled across the bottom.

We just look at it in silence and then look at each other.

'If that's what I think it is, it's over seven hundred years old.' I say with a frown. 'If the Purple Lady was following us yesterday, do you think this is what she was after?'

'If you're worried, you really need to tell your mum. With the work she does at the castle, she'll know what to do. It's a shame though, as she won't let us hang on to the letter and we were starting to get somewhere with our search for Arty's crown.'

'It doesn't have to be over yet,' I say, walking over to the printer, perched on the shelf above the computer. I look up as a flash of movement catches my eye out of the window. But I must be mistaken, because when I look again all I can see is Robin asleep under the bird table - her favourite spot! I continue towards the scanner and, loading the letter, press the green button.

'While you're there can you email it to me, I'd like to check it out later? I have that book on Welsh history that Dad gave me for my birthday.'

'Sure.'

Job done, we go back to the kitchen to find Mum. Just as I thought, she's having the time of her life cleaning out the cupboards to Radio Two, without me under her feet.

'We've a confession to make,' I throw a worried glance in Win's direction. The packet of biscuits was empty, but was there enough chocolate on the top of a McVitie's digestive to make any difference? Perhaps I should have given her my jumbo packet of chocolate buttons that Granny Paddy had given me. Yeah I know, but she still thinks I'm about four – hence the panda slippers! I decide to carry on, regardless of her suspect mood.

'Yesterday, we both thought it was strange the vandals had only caused damage to one part of the tower.' I look at Win again, but he's leaving all the explanations to me. 'So today, while I went to get my pen, I had another look at the wall and I found this.' I hold up the letter.

'I just knew that you were up to no good yesterday. Where exactly did you find this?' She spreads the letter out on the table in front of her.

I go on to tell her about the small hole in the mortar and how I'd excavated it with my pen. I think she's quite impressed, despite herself, as I'm not known for my ingenuity.

'If this is authentic, it's really old and, as sure as buttons open, very very valuable. It could be the reason for the break-in.' She rubs her eyes. 'I suppose I'll have to tell DCI Moreless.'

'DCI who?' I say, only half listening as usual.

'Dai, wake up, would you? The officer that was on your case yesterday.'

'Oh, is that what he's called?' I add, less than interested. I'm not going to make any kind of effort for someone who doesn't like me, even if it is for mum's sake.

'Yeah! I didn't realise it was him at first. I've known Hue for ever. He was in Aunty Patsy's class at school and used to help her with her geography homework.' Mum rambles on, but of course she'd lost us well and truly at humourless. She stalls and just stands there as tears stream down our faces. She just doesn't get it, and we're incapable of telling her. If I'd been writing a book I couldn't have invented a better name for somebody, well for somebody like him. I actually start to feel a little bit sorry for him; no wonder he's so miserable. I thought Dai Monday was a stupid name; his parents must have really hated him.

'I'll have to phone him later, though,' Mum goes on, looking at us both as if we're one button short of a shirt. 'If we don't leave now we're going to be late to meet the train.'

I say a hurried good bye to Win and watch as she rolls up the letter and hides it down the bottom of her knitting bag, covering it with a half-finished rancid green jumper that I'm hoping against hope isn't heading in my direction.

The Robbery

We pull up outside Llandudno Junction station just as the 12.30 from Crewe screeches to a halt, giving me plenty of time to clock that Dad's wearing his yellow and green checked trousers again. You can't miss him, it's what every up and coming Leprechaun about town is wearing these days. I thought, after the last time, Mum was going to hide them down the back of the wardrobe: either she'd forgotten or he's been on the search again. I glance at Sammy to say hello and she half lifts her bejewelled hand in greeting before going back to living inside her headphones. I'd been half thinking of sharing our adventure, but now isn't the time. My mind has already deserted my body, anyway – it's headed back to the lounge, all by itself, to start rummaging through that bag of knitting. All that's needed is for my body to join it - I have to see the letter again.

As soon as Dad stops the car, I leap out, even before he has time to switch off the engine. To cries of 'What's gotten into him?' I make my way to the back door, thinking that this is an unfair gross exaggeration. I can move when I want, all they have to do is press the right buttons: Wii, snack, Wii…

I suddenly lose my train of thought. Something isn't right. The back door is wide open; when I know Mum locked it only half an hour before. Where the lock had been there's now a large gaping hole. I race back to the car to get Dad but, as soon as he sees my face he drops Sammy's bag with a resounding clank of breaking glass before rushing past - breaking glass that sounds and smells a lot like breaking SmellALot!

Don't touch anything.' He digs out his mobile from his back pocket and starts tapping in 999.

I walk inside, hands in my pockets and head straight for the lounge. I just know what I'll find - it doesn't take a genius to add two and two together and come up with four. No one was going to break into a house where there was nothing worth anything.

The beige carpet is now strewn with unravelled green wool, (well, that isn't bad news in itself) where someone had tipped out the contents of mum's knitting bag all over the floor. Robin appears to have added to the disarray, as there's a trail of wool heading back through the hall and out of the cat flap. I think back to earlier, when I thought I'd seen someone in the back garden. They must have been watching us when Mum hid the letter. I look out the window for any sign of Robin, our useless guard cat and notice that something else is missing: the computer. All that's left is a forlorn mouse mat, sitting askew on the top.

Does DCI Humourless ever take any time off? I muse fourteen minutes later when I watch him climb out of his unmarked police car.

When Mum tells him about how I'd found the letter, and that now it's been stolen, his face turns a perfect shade of beetroot. It reminds me of Sammy's latest nail varnish, come to think of it, the one she puts on when Mum's not looking.

He stares at me with angry eyes, and I just know that I'm in for a huge telling off. But, luckily for me, Mum knows what to say.

Sometimes being autistic has its advantages. We're all different, just like we're all special. But being especially different, like me, does mean that grown-ups make allowances. Good old Mum, always on my side, even though I know I cause her a lot of grief. I really do try, but my brain just doesn't work the same as everyone else's. When I get an idea into my head, like disliking red spoons, I just can't focus on anything else. It's as if there's no room for more than one idea at any one time, but boy does that idea get worked through inside out and upside down. Dad's always telling me that, if I could harness this way of thinking, I would be the most successful Welshman ever. Well, apart from Laurence of Arabia, that is. Yeah that's right, not Arabian – Welsh.

I watch on as mum tells him about me, while I decide to act even more weird than usual. They call me *weirdo* at school so this isn't such a hardship. I'd prefer quirky, but whatever - I know it's not true and what I think counts, right? I make a conscious effort to stop blinking and to stare at my fingers - both traits I'm told that emerge when I'm stressed, and if they annoy Humourless the way they annoy everyone else, I'll be let off the hook.

He looks at me for a couple of seconds, and I can see that he isn't going to spend any more of his valuable time on me. I'm dismissed up to my bedroom, which is fine by me, but a big mistake on his part.

Being quirky is no fun, except where brain power is involved and, as Dad keeps telling me, I'm the most intelligent Monday ever.

I reach the landing and, looking left, notice Sammy's door is open for once. She's lying in her usual position; on her tummy, legs swinging backwards and forwards, texting thumbs gliding over her phone quicker than Dad can finish off a pack of digestives behind Mum's back.

Sammy is quite cool, I know that I can be hard work and it is nice to have someone else, that's not an adult, on Team Dai.

I knock on the door and she beckons me into her 'den', as she calls it, or pig sty as it's known to the rest of us. She looks better than usual, no yucky lipstick or mascara, so she's probably not going out later.

I sit down on the edge of her bed and start to tell her everything that has happened over the last twenty-four hours. As her eyes widen, easy without all that mascara, I know I've hooked her. Our adventure is better than an EastEnders plot, any day.

'You're kidding, right? I don't believe it.'

'Believe it, Sis, why do you think someone would break into our house? We must be the only house on the street without a flat screen, and Mum doesn't have any jewellery or anything, does she? You know she's always joking I'm the only 'Dai'mond she owns!'

Brows furrowed, I can see Sammy is struggling to sort things out but, after a minute her face clears.

'Okay, why've you told me all this? Do you need me to help or something?'

Indeed I do. I have a plan and I need a phone that isn't situated in the lounge.

'Sam, how do you fancy joining me around at Win's for a game on the Wii?'

She raises her eyebrows, and I can just guess what she's thinking about having to spend more than five seconds in the company of two stinky ten-year-old boys. But she just shrugs her shoulders and taps in

Buzz's number, before heading downstairs to convince Mum that it would be better for us to go next door while the police are still here.

All three of us are soon installed behind the closed doors of Win's bedroom. Of course, there was never any intention of playing the Wii. Instead, there's absolute silence as we all read the letter that Win has waiting for us.

1284

Dear Sire

During the Excavation for the Castle we have uncovered more bones, we presume from the Abbey. My men have, however, discovered a casket buried alongside these bones. The casket is interesting, fashioned in the shape of a dragon's head with the motto 'Ich dien' carved beneath.

I have hidden the casket for when you next visit.

It is cloaked in a place where only the Great, with hearts forced full of warmth, will have but one chance to find it.

You're faithful Servant
James of St. George

The silence continues as we look at each other. I'm first to break it, but with nothing more challenging than a sigh.

'Well that's about as clear as last week's maths test,' says Sammy - maths not being one of her strong points. Win and I nod in agreement. Where to next?

I pull out my notebook, which is starting to look dog-eared, and add what we've just learnt. I look at the list and then flick back through the other pages.

'So, we know that Arthur is searching for his crown and he wants us to help him.'

Everyone nods in agreement

'The Purple Lady is also looking for something,' Win adds. 'I think she saw the article in the paper. You know, Dai, the one where the twins, whatever they were called, thought the ghost was searching for treasure.'

'And we have to find it first,' Sammy interrupts.

I add to the bottom of my list in bold:

Purple Lady is looking for treasure.

'These clues in the letter, any ideas?' I ask, looking around at the trio of empty faces. 'No nor me. Win, can we borrow your computer?'

With mutual agreement Sammy's nominated as the typist, although with her talons it's a feat (or should that be hand) of engineering for her to even tap the right keys. But that typing course must have included lessons for the digitally challenged as, within a couple of minutes, good old Google has come up trumps again.

Here's what I add to my diary:

Date of letter 1284
To? Most likely Edward 1
From James of St George, Master builder to King Edward
Significance of dragons head: Symbol of Arthur Pendragon. Worn as crest on his crown
Ich dien 'I serve' The motto of the Prince of Wales'

It is cloaked in a place where only the Great with hearts forced full of warmth will have but one chance to find it = No idea.

'Okay, so all we need to find out is who the Purple Lady is and solve the riddle – that's pretty easy, NOT!'

A low rumble interrupts me and I glare at Sammy.

'What! Last thing I had to eat was a plastic sandwich on the train that tasted even worse than it looked.'

Come to think of it, the last thing that I'd eaten was that bacon sandwich, and that was like seven hours ago. I realise all of a sudden just how tired and hungry I am - this day seems to be going on for ever. At least tomorrow is the last day of school before we break up for the Christmas holidays.

When I clamber into bed that night, I notice mum has changed my duvet. Nothing much gets past me; I just choose to ignore most of it. Mind you, no one would notice that I'd different bedding; I'll only have Star Wars so Mum bought me two sets, genius. Although why she had to go and buy those red spoons I'll never know, probably because they were on special at the Co-op.

I lie there, staring at the plain white ceiling and think back over the day. We weren't that much further forward, but at least we'd out-smarted the Purple Lady. I just hope that she hadn't realised we'd also managed to copy the letter - she seemed pretty ruthless. Humourless hasn't found out any more about her, but they're still waiting for the fingerprinting team to report back. He promised to let Mum know so...

The Ghost

The mist is closing in, a cold all-encompassing mist that catches at my breath and makes it painful to breath. I'm standing on the top of the Kings Tower looking out, as rolls upon rolls of fog creep forward on top of the waves in the estuary. The only noise to be heard in the eerie silence is the clinking of the halyards on the yachts moored below. I catch movement out of the corner of my eye and, turning my head, come face to face with King Arthur. This time he's perched on a rock, leaning forward upon the hilt of his large sword. The red eyes are just the same and, just as before, he opens his mouth to speak.

I wake up, gasping for breath, one large droplet of sweat trickling down the back of my neck. It's so cold, but even pulling the duvet further up my neck doesn't stop me from feeling frozen to the core. I open my eyes and find the room as misty as in my dream. I blink a couple of times and reach for my glasses, but the mist remains pooling and stretching before my eyes, just like my worst nightmare.

'What are you doing here? I thought you haunted Conwy Castle?'
'I am King Arthur, please help me.'

If I had skin I could jump out of, I would have! I must still be dreaming, but when I pinch my arm I know that I'm awake. Arthur must have followed me home. How was I going to explain him to Mum at breakfast in the morning? I wonder what he'll make of Rice Krispies going snap, crackle and pop. I decide to go on the defensive. After all, what can a two-thousand-year-old ghost do to me that Greasy Guillim hasn't already tried?

'Okay, okay we've had this conversation before. You're King Arthur and you've lost your crown, right? I'm Dai, nice to meet you,' (even though it wasn't.)

'Dai, I have not lost my crown; it was stolen by Longshanks. It needs to be returned to the last true Princess of Wales, or Britain will never be great again.'

I stare at him. This is getting weird. The last Princess of Wales, but that was Will and Harry's mum, wasn't it? How on earth were we going to manage that? Searching for a crown is one thing, but getting mixed up with royalty? That's off the scale as far as impossible goes. And who or what is Longshanks?

I look at the skinny old man in front of me, with baggy folds of grey skin drooping from his cheeks and I start to feel sorry for him. He reminds me a bit of my granddad.

'King Arthur.'

'Call me Arty, everyone does.'

Everyone, who's everyone? There'd better not be any more like him around, what will Mum say?

'Arty then. You need to help us. Your crown was hidden by King Edward's Master builder, do you know where?'

'Yes, I know all that. Longshanks, or King Edward if you prefer, stole it – do you think I'd be here if I knew where it was?'

'Okay, keep your helmet on. Do you know how big the crown is? What exactly are we looking for?'

'The crown is held within its own silver casket with a crest on top in the shape of a dragon.'

'What size is it?' but he returns my look with a blank stare. 'Well, is it larger than a football?'

'What's a football?'

I look at him, slack jawed. It's useless. How am I meant to hold a conversation with somebody that doesn't have a body and doesn't understand football? I have no idea how they measured in those days. Not metric, but also not in feet and inches unless…I poke my bare foot out from under the duvet.

'How many of my feet long is the casket?'

Not such a silly question then as the reply was quick.

'Two feet long.'

As my feet are about seventeen centimetres in length the box must be about thirty-four centimetres, not too large to be hidden, but where?

I start to yawn. Glancing at my bedside clock, I realise with a shock that it's three o'clock already – these early starts are becoming a bit of a habit – a habit I intend to break, as of now.

'Arty, can you go back home, please? I really need to get some sleep, or I'll be useless in the morning.'

'Dai, I cannot leave your side until the crown is returned. You are my greatest hope.'

If he only knew how stupid that sounds; I'm no one's greatest hope and how am I going to have a wee, with a big, see-through, ghoul looking over my shoulder?

'Okay King, er, Arty, but you're going to have to wait in the lounge. I'm never going to get to sleep with you here, and I'm not going anywhere being as I'm only ten.

'What's a lounge?'

This wasn't getting any easier. I look from him to my bed in exasperation. If I didn't think of something pretty quick, I wouldn't be getting any more sleep tonight. My eyes shift to the chair beside my bed as a light bulb explodes within my mind.

'Arty, we have a great hall downstairs, on the left, with a large green padded throne, please avail yourself of it freely, I'll come and get you in the morning.' With that, Arty starts to fade before my eyes.

I climb into my now cold bed, shivering with fear as well as the plummeting temperature. Pulling the duvet up to my ears, in case of further unwanted ghostly apparitions, I wait for sleep, which seems a long time coming.

I have more to worry about than spoons in the morning. I race downstairs as soon as I hear Dad singing in the shower; although why he always sings 'It's raining men' I'll never know. I don't have much time - I can already hear mum putting on the kettle. But still I hesitate, my hand poised on the door handle to the lounge. I wonder what I'll find. I wonder if he'll still be there. I expect the lounge to be empty. I don't believe in ghosts more than that, especially ones that pop round for a chat during the small hours.

I've pretty much convinced myself that last night was a dream, and a very silly one at that - feet and foot indeed! I look around and heave a sigh of relief - that is until I walk towards the fireplace to find him curled up asleep on the sofa. He hasn't even bothered to take his boots off, but I suppose that doesn't matter – invisible germs shouldn't be that much of a problem.

Mum comes in then and gives a little scream. 'What's wrong? Why are you up so

early? I don't know what's gotten into everyone today. Robin's been meowing

outside the lounge for half the night. If I didn't know better, I'd think we had mice.'

Yeah right, a whopping huge rodent!

She rambles on as only mothers can, not expecting me to listen or anything. I stare at her open-mouthed - she must be able to see Arty, but clearly not as she's just thrown a cushion at his head. He sits up, scratching his tummy under his tunic and its then I decide it's probably best not to say anything. She'd only take me straight back to that child psychologist to answer another book full of daft questions. I run out of the room, mumbling something about getting ready for school and, of course, Arty follows, well it's more of a glide. It must be cool not having to bother with doors.

After gathering my clothes together and leaving Arty mooching around my room, I volunteer for a shower. Only to have five minutes privacy to get dressed, but Dad isn't to know that. So now both parents think I'm seriously loopy, not just one.

On my return, I wish I hadn't left him alone; my room looks like a bomb's hit it. My clock radio's blaring and Arty has disappeared. No, wait a minute; is that his sword peeking out from under my bed? I bend down and there he is, huddled as far back against the wall as he can get, oblivious to the old smelly sock that's only inches away from his nose. I let out a snort of annoyance - I've been looking for that sock for ages.

'There's magic afoot. You must be a very powerful wizard to make that box talk.' He leans across and pats me on the back. 'I'll have to ask Merlin to pop by so you can tell him some of your secret spells.'

My jaw drops to the floor: Magic box? Merlin Where? What? Then my eyes snag on my clock radio still blaring out Kylie, and everything clicks into place. Explaining about the lounge was one thing, but making a box talk and sing was something else. He'd never believe me if I told him the truth, and what was the truth anyway? It would take months to explain how man had evolved and progressed across the centuries, the culmination being the ability to hear Kylie blast out La La La at top volume across the country.

I know there's no such thing as magic. You know there's no such thing as magic - but I don't want him conjuring up Merlin just to prove us both wrong! Perhaps it would be easier to just let him think that indeed I am a powerful wizard – ha!

At least breakfast isn't going to be a problem. Once I've turned off the talking box there is no opposition to my suggestion that he stays in my room. Arty has told me that ghosts can't eat. However, they do have an acute sense of smell, which makes the smell of food unbearable. The same probably goes for a whiff of one of my socks. Oh well…I consider that to be payback for my 3 am wake-up call.

But the rest of the morning doesn't turn out to be as easy. Have you ever tried getting a two-thousand-year-old ghost into a car? I ended up having to coax him by explaining it was a magical four-horse power carriage and this in front of Mum too. Of course, to her it must have looked like I'd lost the plot, what with getting out of bed on time, volunteering for a shower and now talking to myself. But I don't have a choice…

'Instead of our horses eating hay, they guzzle their way through a special super food called diesel,' I add, hoping to appear more knowledgeable than I feel.

When we eventually pull up outside school, Arty hangs back, but that's not surprising. Tons of kids streaming through the doors is a daunting prospect for me, let alone someone who has more wrinkles than a squashed prune.

'I will just wait for you here, Dai,' he says, plonking down on the top step, his sword sticking out at a right angle just ready to trip up any unsuspecting ghost. I nudge it out of the way with my foot before sitting down beside him.

'I can't make you come with me. I know it must seem scary, but this may be your only chance ever to go to school. I find going to school frightening.' Arty looks unconvinced, but I carry on. 'Some of the boys and a fair few of the girls too, come to think of it, are nasty to Win and me. They chase us; they hit us and trash our belongings. But they can't take away the fact that some of the teachers are great and we learn about some really cool stuff. This may be your only chance and you may live to regret it.' My voice peters out.

Does Arty realise that he's dead? Surely he must do, but he's probably more worried about all the neat stuff he's missing out on, like sausages and chips, or whatever it was they used to eat in those days. I half expect him to turn around and walk down the steps again; instead he just glides past me into the building, his head held high.

'Monday.'

I stop at the sound of my name and turn around to face the headmaster. He's the only one that calls me Monday, all the rest of the teachers are happy to bellow out 'Die' at the top of their voices, but not him. I wonder what I've done, or not done this time.

'Monday - this is Stuart Pitt, he'll be joining your class for the day and I would like you to look after him.'

Really? I glance across at the sullen-looking giant in mute horror. He towers over everything in sight - surely he has to be older than ten? He is even a head taller than the Head.

Something's wrong. I can feel it – someone is watching me. You know that funny feeling you get when all the hairs at the back of your neck stand to attention? My gaze shifts across to the woman leaning against the door jamb, her cold calculating eyes glued to me with undisguised hostility.

This woman clearly didn't like me but…my heart drops to my regulation black lace-ups. There is no mistaking those thunder thighs, this time squeezed into a too small pair of jeans with the seams stretched so tight that the stitching is visible. I kind of guessed she'd be popping up, as well as popping out again but I hadn't reckoned on it happening quite so soon. She mustn't have solved the riddle yet, and her being here must mean she thinks we know more than she does.

I'm in trouble.

Greasy Guillim was one thing, but this Stu Pitt is out of his league. I turn to speak to Arty, but he's nowhere to be seen – he'd disappeared with perfect timing. I am on my own.

'Sir, I don't know that I am the right person to…' I begin.

'Of course you are, Monday, look at the wonders you've done with Bee,' he interrupts.

Stu sniggers, until his mum sorts him out with a kick to the shins.

I start to open my mouth, but close it at the sight of the headmaster turning away, taking the Purple Lady with him. There is still no sign of Arty, there's no sign of anybody except 'Stupid' standing in front of me, chewing gum. I've never felt more alone in someone else's company. But I have no choice other than to follow orders and lead him to our classroom - at least nothing can happen in a crowded corridor.

I'm wrong. As soon as we're out of sight, Stupid grabs my arm in a vice-like hold and starts to squeeze it like a tube of toothpaste.

'Where's the treasure, you little titch. You'd better tell me or you'll be for it.' I look down and see his grubby, nail-bitten hands clawing around my arm, the knuckles straining against the skin. He's wearing a large silver ring on his index finger and the pain from that hurts most of all. Where is everyone? This part of the school is always teeming at this time, but just like Arty, everyone seems to have disappeared. They are probably too scared, and I can't blame them. I feel his fingers dig even deeper into my flesh, even as I feel my eyes sting from the tears that are building up against my eyelids.

Please don't cry. It's always worse when you cry.

The bone crushing pain is unbearable, anymore and he'd break my arm. It is hard to continue walking, any movement in my arm and he squeezes even tighter. When is this pain going to end?

If I knew anything, I'd tell him, an injured arm isn't going to help anybody, least of all me. I'm just about to collapse with the pain when he lets go so quickly that I stumble onto my knees.

I just stay there, the hard floor digging into my skin and feel relief. I want to cradle my arm like a toddler. I want to examine it for any damage, but most of all I want to make the pain go away. The tears I'd struggled to hold back start trickling down my face unchecked. The worst thing of course is that, whilst I hate Stupid for hurting me, I hate myself more for not stopping him. If only I'd had the courage to call out for help. If only I'd had the courage to stand up to the headmaster…Even now, with the immediate threat of pain out of the way I know that I'm going to chicken out and do nothing.

I'm not going to fight, I not going to get my own back. I'm not going to squeal to the Head. I'm going to do exactly what I'm doing now – a big fat nothing.

I sit at the bottom of the stairs trying and failing to sniff back my tears. That is until some part of me wonders why he'd stopped. I force my eyes to open, just in case it's a trap but it's not. He's just standing a few feet away, staring around with his jaw trailing the floor. Even as I try to figure out what's happening, he glances down at his trousers and then back at me, confusion stamped all over his face. I see him shake his head in disbelief before walking into our classroom.

I start after him, but only because I have no choice. I can't afford to be kept after school and kept away from the riddle. Now if Arty had been there to help instead of running away I'm sure things would have been different.

I reach the door to find my way barred by him, a big silly grin scrawled across his face.

'What have you been up to Arty? I could really have used a hand back there.'

'Oh, this and that,' he says. 'Have you hurt your arm?'

'It's nothing.'

'No, Dai, it's not nothing. I saw what he did to you. Don't worry, he won't harm you again.'

I stare at him, standing there, looking so cool with his cloak and sword. I want to believe everything he says, but I just can't. No adult has been able to help Win and me before, so why should now be any different?

'Whatever. I have to go, or I'll be late for class and it's bad enough as it is.'

Stupid

I sit down beside Win with a sigh. I can sense his eyes peering at me, but I keep my face averted. I'm too ashamed of my still damp face, just as I'm too ashamed of being a loser, yet again. Win has been in the same spot too many times not to understand that I need to be alone, even in this crowded classroom.

That's another thing about me - I can switch off the outside as easily as most people can switch off a light bulb. I have lots to think about, and nothing that is going on in the classroom is relevant at the moment. My thoughts are fluttering around in my head like leaves in the wind. The one central truth is I have to solve that riddle. I have to solve that riddle and stay away from Stupid and Guillim while I do it - both of whom are sitting in the back row, as thick as thieves.

Win breaks into my thoughts with a sly nudge to the ribs and I look up. Everyone has started to take notes from the white board on the school project for the Christmas holidays. I open my history book and one percent of my brain follows suit, whilst the other ninety nine percent continues to work out how I'm going to avoid Stupid and Guillim for the rest of the day. I could hang around with Win during break, but that would only involve him.

What about Arty? Could he help? I look up, scanning the room. Yes, there he is, lounging on the window-sill beside Froggy's geranium. He's staring at her with a rapt expression on his face; all very worrying considering that Miss Froggitt is called Froggy for a reason. Perhaps he's in need of some glasses, although do ghosts wear glasses or...? Miss Froggitt's voice interrupts my thoughts.

'Dai Monday, as you've been staring out the window for the last five minutes, you must have already got your holiday history project underway?'

I turn my head back to the classroom, and my brain follows with some quick thinking.

'Yes, Miss.'

She stares at me, one eyebrow arched in disbelief. 'Really? Well, if you can take the time out of your busy schedule, we are all waiting with bated breath.'

'Er, I've decided to put together the family tree for AP Gruffudd, the Last Welsh Prince of Wales.' Not bad, even for me.

Froggy's gaze holds mine. 'I look forward to your presentation with great anticipation,' she retorts. 'As you seem to have your strategy planned, you can miss break and help me sort out the computer room.'

She looks even more suspicious at the sight of the huge grin breaking across my face, but I can't hide my happiness at the sight of Stupid's horrified expression. I feel as if I've just escaped the firing squad, even though I'll be missing out on playing footie on the Astro.

I hang back after class, taking my time to gather my stuff together. With Win beside me and Stupid safely out of the way, I decide to ask Miss Froggitt for advice. She's okay most of the time - another adult on Team Dai.

'Miss, I was wondering if I could ask you something, please?'

'Yes Dai.' She stops writing in her diary and looks up.

'We're trying to puzzle out this riddle and we aren't getting very far.' I put my hand in the pocket of my school shorts and hand over a crumpled-up piece of paper.

She looks at the paper for a second before meeting my gaze. 'Word puzzles are written in ways to trick the reader. You need to deconstruct the sentence and concentrate on each word for possible meanings. It's not too long, so it should be easy for a couple of bright boys like you two,' she adds, smiling as she hands it back. 'Now hurry along to games, or you'll be late.' She stares at me, her eyes wide. 'You're all right, are you, Dai? None of the boys annoying you?'

I shake my head. There's no way she knows about Stupid, is there? I glance around for Arty, but he's done another disappearing act.

'Well, you know you can always come to me.' She turns and focuses a bright blue-eyed glare across at Win, who's standing by my side. 'Don't forget you're helping me later, and bring Win – it'll be quicker with the three of us, and I'll be able to keep an eye on you both.'

No further forward, but at least Win is safe for the moment, too. With Arty, shadow hopping behind us, we make our way to the changing room.

Win rolls his eyes. 'Did you have to bring him along? He looks a bit out of place here.'

'I had no choice,' I whisper back. 'I think it's just you and me that can see him. He turned up last night at home, scared me out of my wits, I can tell you.'

Moments later, changing into my football jersey, I have the first opportunity to check out my arm. It still hurts, but now it feels more like a dull throb. The skin is stained a dullish grey where a hand-shaped bruise is forming. In the centre is a deep red indentation in the shape of a dragon, a red dragon.

Arty stands on the side lines in his element as he watches his first ever football match. Win and I sit on the subs bench, hunched over our knees trying to work out the puzzle - for once, the safest and luckiest place to be. When, thirty minutes into the second half, we're called as token substitutes, I try to stay well back from any play but, being cautious isn't enough to protect me. I thought I'd be safe on a crowded football pitch.

Big mistake.

The ball comes out of nowhere like a torpedo, and hits my stomach with the force of ten donkeys. It's strong enough to knock me off my feet and it's strong enough to wind me. I rest my head back against the cold blades of grass, trying to work out which part hurts the most. My stomach aches, my head aches and my arm aches. I must have hit my head, losing consciousness, because the next thing I know, Stupid's bending over me. I try to shout for help, but the only noise I make sounds like a constipated horse. He's kneeling beside me, pretending to apologise, pretending to look sorry while all the time he's crushing my already injured arm.

'Thought any more about the riddle yet? My mum really needs to know,' he says softly, so softly that only I can hear.

I'm still dazed – I must be. I can't believe he'd have the nerve to try and injure me for a second time, and in front of an audience too.

What does he have to gain and, more to the point what can I tell him that would stop the pain? I don't know anything. I haven't worked out the riddle, and I don't even know if I ever will. My eyes start to sting, but this time I'm determined not to cry. After all, there is only so much damage he can inflict before the referee comes over to check on me. I lie back and try to focus on the sharp blades of grass piercing my skin like needles, even as I start counting in my head. It should only take about sixty seconds for the ref to appear. I only get to eleven when the sound of laughter erupts from the crowd, interrupting me.

Great, there's me in absolute agony, and everyone thinks it's funny. As the laughter grows, Stupid lets go of my arm. I sneak a look and then smile at the sight of his shorts around his ankles, and then I laugh – well, so would you.

I'm not laughing at his shorts, I'm laughing at the sight of his boxers, still visible as he frantically scrabbles around to drag his shorts back in place - his pink boxers dotted with little blue and yellow embroidered flowers – he looks absolutely ridiculous.

I manage to sit up just in time to see him run away from the jeering crowd before turning to Arty, who's magically appeared out of nowhere.

'I told him earlier that he had strange taste in underwear. I don't think he'll be bothering you any more, Dai.'

Arty has just saved me for the second time today. Now it's my turn to save him, if I can. The only problem is; I still haven't come up with any ideas for the riddle yet. But at least Stupid is sorted for the moment. I can live with a sore arm and a headache.

After being released by the school nurse, I head outside to find Mum waiting for me at the school gates, as is The Purple Lady. Mum looks pretty much as usual in her jeans and hair pulled off her face with a bit of string, so I focus my attention on the vision in tight purple on her left - and man, what a vision! It's almost uncanny, how much she looks like a pig with her rosy red cheeks and multiple chins that rival Mr Fothergill's colossal neck. I take in her jeans and bulging top, and I count my blessings that Mum is Mum and not her, if you know what I mean.

Dad used to say that she looked best by candlelight – that is until she lost it and gave his sirloin to Robin. She wrapped it up in a smart tale about the cat jumping on the kitchen counter, but Sammy and I know the truth. We'd laughed ourselves silly at the sight of his face when he saw what was for tea – one of Sammy's veggie sausages!

'Good looking woman that.'

I nearly jump out of my shoes at the sound of Arty's voice whispering in my ear. 'Who?' My gaze is still fixed on the Purple Lady. Surely he couldn't...?

'Your Mum, of course. All that wild untamed red hair...'

'Auburn! She'll kill you if you call her a redhead.'

'Er, that might be quite difficult,' he says with a laugh, a big goofy smile on his face.

Whilst Mum looks pleased to see me, the Purple Lady looks furious. The last I glimpse of her angry face is as she screeches away in her white, beaten-up van.

Instead of answering the usual *'How was your day?'* I hijack the conversation with my own line of cross examination. She wouldn't believe me anyway; bullies in pink boxers and ghosts that would soon be progressing to wedgies if current trends continue.

'Have you heard from Humour...Officer Moreless today, Mum? Any news about the break-ins?'

She doesn't answer, but that's understandable as the last time I distracted her at the school gates she ended up running over the Lollypop Man's foot.

'I was going to wait till we got home. Hue phoned me earlier. They found a match for one of the sets of fingerprints in the Castle. It looks like we were right after all and that it was just vandals.'

I glance at Arty, sitting quietly in the passenger seat. 'Really?'

'Yes, the fingerprints belong to a sixteen-year-old boy. He's known to the police for some minor offence in the past, thieving from a shop or something.'

I just don't believe it, it doesn't make sense. I was so sure that the treasure was the key.

'Hold on a minute, Mum. You said one of the sets, how many were there?'

'Just two. Funny though - the second set of finger prints was the same as those found at home. Must be a coincidence.'

Coincidences like that just don't happen, but she's not to know that and I'm not going to tell her – she's had enough worries over the last two days to last a lifetime.

'Did Officer Moreless tell you any more about the boy?' I ask. 'It wouldn't have been an antique shop that he stole from?'

'Well, actually.' She pauses, turning in her seat to look me straight in the eye. 'Dai Monday, what are you not telling me? This isn't child's play you know, someone could get hurt.'

But she's lost me as soon as she's confirmed my worse fear. I knew that Stu was older, but sixteen years old! What was the school playing at? I could have been injured, or worse. Wait until I tell Win.

I don't know what to do so I sit back, rubbing my arm and my stomach, both of which are still throbbing from the battering they'd had. I now knew what a pickle Win and I are in. The Purple Lady and her psycho son meant business.

'Mum, I don't feel very well. When we get home can you phone Officer Moreless,

I've some information about the Purple Lady that I think he needs to know.'

I close my eyes in an effort to shut out my thoughts, but it's no good. I can't stop myself thinking about Stupid and just how stupid the headmaster had been not to check his age. Being bullied by ten-year-olds was bad enough, but sixteen was as good as grown up! I try to blank my mind and concentrate on the puzzle, but all I can think about is the debt I owe Arty and how I'm probably never going to be able to repay him.

Following a difficult conversation with old Humourless, it materialises that Stu's mother did indeed own an Antique shop in Rhyl, and was well known for her dishonest dealings, not that they could pin anything on her. In fact, word had it that she's the main receiver of stolen goods in the North Wales area. With a warrant out for her arrest, I feel a lot more secure - the only thing left is that wretched puzzle.

The Riddle

We are all lounging around in Win's room, full of chocolate donuts instead of ideas. Win is flicking through one of his history books, while I'm just standing by the window, my brain trying to untangle the riddle. Sammy's with us, for once, but not so anyone would notice. Apart from the tinny sounds emitting from her headphones, the only other noise is the rustling of pages. As for King Arthur, he's sitting cross-legged on the bed just staring at the floor.

'What happens if we can't find your crown then, Arty?' says Win, as he closes his last history book with a snap and adds it to the large pile on the floor beside him.

'Nothing, things will just carry on as before. I'll go back to haunting the Castle. But I'm really bored of that, if I have to say boo just once more, I'll scream.' He scratches the back of his head. 'Actually that's not a bad idea; I could add it to my repertoire.'

'And what happens if we do find it?'

'It needs to be with the last Welsh Princess of Wales,' he says with a small smile.

Sammy glances up. 'Yeah, but how are we going to achieve that? That's like royalty, right?'

I press my hot forehead against the cool window pane in a desperate need of inspiration. My eyes focus on the English and Welsh flags wafting in the breeze as I try to work it out. I knew the last Welsh Prince of Wales was that bloke – Gruff something. I'd know a lot more about him when I started on my history project, but who was the last Princess? I open the rucksack slumped by my feet and pull out my trusty notebook. Old Gruff must have had a kid.

'Win, can you do a search on Google, we need to find out whether Al Gruffolo had any kids?'

Arty gives me a piercing look. 'Do you mean AP Gruffudd by any chance? There's no point in searching Goggleys, is it?' he says with a frown. 'You don't need any new-fangled devices when you have me. I have been around since forever; ever since the bones of my great great great great great great great grand-son were laid to rest in 1282.'

I stop peering at my notebook and peer at him instead.

'Yes that's right: AP was my relation and now I want to find my great great great great great great great great grand-daughter, who was stolen away from her true destiny.' He heaves a big sigh, before turning his attention to his left big toe that's poking out through a hole in his thick woollen sock.

'I know you and Win are having a really tough time with the boys at the school, but sometimes it's not just children that can be horrible. My little Gwen lost her mum when she was born.' He throws a quick glance at Win's suddenly still profile. 'Then when she was a few weeks old her dad and uncle were killed. Afterwards Gwen, the last Welsh Princess of Wales, was stolen and taken off Welsh soil; I know not where, but Britain will never be great until the Welsh crown is returned...'

'Yeah, Yeah! Okay we know the last part. That's not as awkward as Will and Harry's mum then,' piped up Sammy. 'All we need to do is find where little Gwen is buried.'

'AND find out where the crown is?' Win adds. 'We can't forget about the search for his crown and we aren't getting very far with that. We might as well just tear up the letter now and burn it in the grate, for all the good it's doing us.'

Something tingles in the recesses of my brain as the synapses start firing up. The electric currents make the hairs on the back of my neck stand to attention. Grates, Greats, Heart, hearths.

'Can you say that again, but more slowly, please.' I drag out the crumpled slip of paper from my pocket.

Win glares at me as if I've suddenly grown another head. 'Well, I said about burning it in the grate, not that that's relevant.' He points to his empty fireplace, 'Dad wouldn't let me use the fireplace in a month of Mondays!'

I ignore the joke, it isn't his best.

'Look, what if.' I stall, not really sure if what I'm about to say will make any sense. 'What if the Great meant the Great Hall – as in the fireplace in the Great Hall?'

Arty leaps off the bed and starts jumping around the room like a demented two-year-old with a full nappy.

'That's it. You're brilliant I knew you would solve it. Let's go now and claim my crown.'

I look around at the sea of smiling faces and can't stop my face grinning back. If this is the answer, it'll get Stupid off our backs, and keep Win happy for weeks. And then I remember that going to the castle is going to be difficult, especially now.

'It's not as easy as that, I'm afraid.' I glance down at my watch. 'The Castle closes in like half an hour and it will still be crawling with coppers. We're not going to get a chance to examine the fireplace in peace.'

We look at each other, defeated at the last hurdle.

We'd just have to pass this all over to Old Humourless, it would be sure to put him in a good mood, NOT.

'Didn't you say your mum was stock taking tonight?' Win sat bolt upright.

'Yeah, she'll be home by seven. Dad has to cook supper so it's bound to be cheese and tomato pizza again.'

'Well, why don't we go and join her and see if we can give her a hand?' Sammy interrupts.

'You must be joking? She'd smell a rat, straight off. There are no flies on Mum; you should know that - you have known her four years more than me!'

'But there's not much she can do if we're already there, and she doesn't know I'm involved, now does she?'

'Okay, that's a point.' I turn to Win. 'What do you think, buddy?'

'Let's give it a go. She can only turn us away and we won't have lost anything, except an hour in front of the telly.'

I stand up and start to cram my notebook back into my rucksack.

'That's a good idea.' Sammy races out of the room, nearly tripping over Arty's size ten's in the process. Seconds later, she's returned with her rucksack slung over her shoulder. The twin of mine, buy one get second one half price at the Co-op, another one of Mum's bargains. I suppose I should be thankful that they're boring blue and not covered in flowers, like Stupid's pants.

I look at Sammy, eyebrows raised. Sammy doesn't do notebooks, unless she has to. 'Well, Mum may smell a pack of rats but, with a flask of tea and one of those donuts left over from earlier, it will be difficult for her to give us a hard time.'

My sister, for all her faults, does have some cool ideas, I would never have thought of that in a year of Monday's.

If anyone had seen the funny procession of three kids, and a ghost heading towards the castle they'd have run down the high street screaming like a banshee. Win and I lead the way, but it's the vision of Arty, carrying my sister's bulging bag in one hand and his sword in the other that is the scariest. It doesn't help that Sammy has decided to throw in the fruit bowl, just in case Mum is having one of her 'fat' days, although I do think she should have left the actual dish at home.

When we arrive at the visitor's centre, Mum is just locking up after the last tourist, and is in the process of heading back to count pots. She does indeed smell a whole sewer of rats, but the sight of Sammy seems to calm her. Either that or the sight of the chocolate covered donut with extra sprinkles. Fat day or not, I knew I wouldn't get as much as a crumb.

Sammy winks, before asking if we can wait in the Great Hall - that way we won't be able to get into any trouble. She nods her head and goes back to counting the ugly teapots on the top shelf.

By the time we arrive, darkness has long since enveloped the chamber. It's empty and silent, apart from the gardeners cart full of brushes and rakes for the paths in the morning. I've never seen it without visitors trawling around and it feels cold, eerie and frankly a bit frightening. At least we remembered our torches, all except for Arty that is, but who's ever heard of a ghost that needs a torch – that would be silly.

In silent agreement, we all head for the fireplace, the focal point of the whole room. I drop my rucksack beside Sammy's and kneel down to inspect the stones.

Been there, done that, but after fifteen minutes of inspecting each brick and fissure there's no sign of any T-Shirt, or to be more exact not a whiff of any crown. There's nothing to see. Each brick is boringly the same as its neighbour with no cracks, no holes and no place to hide anything. We continue examining the fireplace for another four minutes, but this time there is no magical Eureka moment - just sore knees and grazed hands. Eventually I sit on the ground, still rubbing my knees. I pull out the letter, for what must be the fiftieth time and stare down at the words that, in truth, I can recite with my eyes closed and my hands tied behind my back. The words stare silently back, but if there are any clues hiding in their depths, they aren't sharing.

With a sudden jerk, Win leaps forward and grabs it out of my hand, ripping it in two.

'Hey, mind what you're doi…'

'Dai, Dai hang on a minute.' He stands over me, his eyes gleaming like beacons from the reflected torch light. 'When it says, 'Hearts full of Warmth,' do you think that the grate should have a fire in it?'

I look up into his face, part of me annoyed, angry even, that he's gone and done it again. He's gone and beaten me to it. I'd so wanted to be the one to solve the mystery. But the other part, the larger part, is just happy to see my best friend happy – happier than I've ever seen him before.

'Okay, great idea, but how are we going to light a fire, any ideas?'

He shakes his head as reality hits. We've come so far, only to fail for the want of a miserable match.

'Hold on.' Sammy starts to rummage in the front pocket of her rucksack before pulling out a rumpled packet of fags, a sheepish expression on her face.

'Dad's going to have a canary.'

'It's alright,' she interrupts.' I've only smoked a couple, everyone is doing it, but I don't like them. Here.' She thrusts them into my hands. 'You take the packet, there's a lighter inside.'

There is nothing to burn until I remember my notebook. I rip the blank pages out from the back before crumpling them and placing them in the centre of the grate.

'Here Win, this was your idea.' I hold out the lighter.

We all stand around watching the paper touch the tip of the flame, mesmerised by the glowing yellow, red and orange flames curling upwards towards the sky. I know now that the last few days have been building up to something momentous and this is it the moment of truth. We don't know what to expect. Would a brick pop open to reveal a secret hiding place? Would there be a secret passage, or would there be a magic door? After a minute of watching we finally get what we don't expect.

Nothing!

Banana

Nothing happens.

There was nothing to see. No magic. No tricks - just a big fat nothing. We all glance at each other, the disappointment reflected on all of our faces. We've tried and failed. That's it, no more ideas. Maybe the crown has already been discovered, although surely Arty would have known?

We all watch the flames diminish to a dull glow before petering out, until all that's left is a little pile of cold grey cinders in the middle of the grate. King Arthur looks on silently. We can all see the devastation etched across his face – it seems as if he's aged another century in the last five minutes. And who could blame him? His last hope lay smashed into a thousand pieces in the middle of the cooling embers in front of us.

Sammy breaks through our sad reverie, as common sense kicks in.

'Dai, can you fetch that dustpan and brush from the gardener's cart? Mum will freak if she finds out we've lit a fire in here.'

They say girls turn into their mothers. When we get home I wouldn't be surprised if she scrubs her face clean, chops off her Hollywood nails and goes downstairs to peel some vegetables, or whatever it is that mother's actually do in the kitchen.

I watch, without seeing, as she starts to sweep up the now cool ashes. My mind isn't in the Great Hall; it's backtracking over all of our steps in an effort to spot where we'd gone wrong. I'd been so certain that we'd been onto something, but there are no secrets hidden here, no hidde…

'Hold on, Sammy, wait up! I snatch the brush, causing her to land on her bum with a yelp. But it doesn't matter – all that matters is the strange pattern in the middle of the grate.

Moments later, I've scraped away the remainder of the ashes and we all stand back to stare at the ground.

Where before there had only been blank stone, now the ash from the fire has settled into the grooves to reveal a pattern. Someone has engraved feint markings, as clear as a map, onto the smooth, hard surface.

It is then I remember Win. Without him we wouldn't be here.

'Sammy, let Win look - it was his idea to light the fire, remember.'

We step back to let him kneel by the fireplace and run his hands over the still warm stone.

'It's not just scratches, but it's not words either. Look, here's a faint line with a triangle at one end. An arrow, do you think? And here, underneath some numbers, not letters, encased in rectangles, one vertical and one horizontal,' he adds, 'and look, a picture.'

I join him and see what he sees. 'The numbers look like a two and a four and I think that may be a drawing of a dragon. Arty, what do you think?'

Arty's expression is cautiously optimistic. He's been disappointed too many times in the past to think that this time will be any different. But his voice can't hide his excitement as he joins us in staring at the floor.

'Yes, that's it. My little Dragon! At last, I can smell my crown, it's so close now.'

Arty suddenly disappears. I'm staring at him one second, and the next I'm staring at the wall behind. Very pecul…

Something or someone lifts me off the ground and flings me across the floor. And then I see the hand - the hand with the grubby, nail-bitten fingers and the same silver ring in the shape of a dragon.

Oh no, we'd been concentrating so hard we hadn't heard them creep up on us. Arty must have spotted them first and that's why he's disappeared.

'Wh…what are you doing here? The castle closed ages ago'.

The Purple Lady's small black eyes glare at me, a huge smile pulling at her thin lips. 'We hid in the dungeon, while the tourists were being rounded up. What are you doing over there, what are you all looking at, what have you found?' She pushes Win out of the way and heads for the fireplace.

We remain silent, not wanting to help them in any way. I can't believe our luck, or more accurately lack of. I had thought the Welsh constabulary would have rounded up this pair long ago, but obviously not. As part of me wonders idly where they've been holed up, the rest of my brain carries on working out the puzzle.

An arrow pointing to the wall behind us. Rectangles that represent bricks. Vertical for rows up and horizontal for rows across; just like, just like the coordinates on a map. Bingo. How clever, but also how simple. King Edward's master-builder had made us a map. He must have been an utter genius. But, it turns out very quickly that I'm not.

As soon as I've solved the puzzle, a smile breaks out. I just can't help it. Win and me, two awkward and quirky Welsh boys have solved something no one else has been able to.

'Mum, Mum, look at Dai. He knows something.'

'Then make him talk, what are you waiting for?'

I watch, eyes unable to look anywhere other than at Stupid's head as he comes towards me with grimy outstretched hands. I try not to think about what he's going to do because, as sure as balls bounce, it's going to hurt. Whatever it is, I just know I don't have the strength to fight any more. I hope Sammy and Win will understand and won't think me too much of a coward. There is only so much a ten-year-old can take.

I am a weak nerd. I know this because everyone at school, apart from Win, has spent the last five years telling me. It's not good enough that I'm both kind and smart - if you're not part of the pack; you're nobody, an outsider. It's like being at a party you haven't been invited to, and there have been plenty of those over the years.

'Stop.' I hold up my hand and point. 'You need to check out that wall over there –

second brick up, fourth brick along.'

I feel something touch my arm. It's Sammy – she's taken my hand. It's strange; strangely reassuring so I don't shake her off, for once. No one likes to be a coward, but perhaps in my position she'd have done the same. Who knows. I give her a reassuring little smile, just to let her know I'm okay, even as I promise myself that I'm not going to tell Dad about the smoking. We're all allowed one error of judgement – this is her freebie.

We all watch them rush over to the opposite wall and, after much dithering, find the right brick. They push, prod and tap for what seems like ages, but nothing – this pair is a real pair of dim watts. We've handed it to them on a plate and they still can't work it out. At least they can't see Arty peering over their shoulders shaking his head. That would have really cheered them up.

'Alright you, clever clogs,' she says, looking straight at me. 'You have sixty seconds to work this out, or I'll set my son on your friend.'

Having less choice than you find in a packet of chocolate buttons, I walk over to join the happy duo.

But first I glance at my watch.

OKAY, I know, so don't go on already - now is not the time for watch gazing. But sixty seconds isn't long and I'm pretty sure they won't let me start my stop watch. I drop my arm and resort to desperate measures.

ONE BANANA

TWO BANANA

I start to examine the brick in front of me. At first I can't see anything either: just an uneven sand-coloured block with roughened edges, amongst a sea of other similar blocks.

FIVE BANANAS

Hold a banana though; all the other bricks adjacent to it are more of a reddish colour. It's as if someone has iced the brick, but with sand instead of icing. Why would they have covered the bricks unless…

EIGHT BANANAS

'Win, can you hand me over that brush, please?' I point over my shoulder to the brush lying discarded beside the grate.

I start brushing and, as I brush, clumps of sand fall away, revealing the little carved figure of a dragon.

There's absolute silence in the Great Hall that is apart from Arty breathing down the back of my neck. In a funny sort of way, it's good to have him so close. He's turning into a bit of a lucky mascot as far as I'm concerned. Of course, he can't do much to help, but at least he's right up there supporting me - in fact, if he gets any closer he might as well stand in my shoes.

But what next? I waste precious bananas just staring at the cute little engraving while I try to work out what it all means. What am I meant to do now? It isn't as if the dragon has an arrow that says 'Start digging here.' My heart drops to my feet as I see Stu walking towards me and I still don't know what to do.

'Get on with it, will yah.'

Get on with what, you big lummox? If I knew what to get on with, don't you think I would?

I turn to face Win; he always knows what to do.

'Think back to the puzzle, Dai – you only have one chance to get it right, the answer must be in front of you.'

The puzzle, right. I must concentrate on the puzzle, and try and forget the big buffoon looming behind me. I've read it so many times I don't even have to look at the paper...'

Stupid pushes me for a second time, only harder. So hard that I can feel the imprint of his hand across my shoulders. So hard that for once in my life I lose it.

It isn't fair! Here we are, trying to help and he isn't even giving me time to think. An unexpected heat builds up inside me, as fierce as if I've swallowed ten cups of cocoa. For the first time ever, I know what it means to have steam coming out of your ears. All the injustices of the last few days appear before my eyes just as clearly as if someone has pressed high speed rewind. It isn't right, it isn't fair and I am not going to put up with it any longer. I've had enough of both him and his mother, thank you very much. I square my shoulders, all of the anger exploding like a volcano.

How dare they? They've won, haven't they? Yet they are still shouting, still yelling and still pushing; just like Greasy Guillim and his gang. Well, this boy is not a victim of bullying anymore. I take a step forward and, even though my chin only reaches his chest, I give him a mighty great push, with all the force from the last five years tucked quietly behind it.

The one word for the look on Stupid's face is surprise. He looks surprised as he loses his balance and falls against the wall with a loud thud, and he looks even more surprised when I kneel down beside him and start bellowing in his left ear.

'If you ever speak to me, or touch me like that again, you'll be for it.' I tell him, my voice flat. 'There are three of us against you and,' I point to his mother, 'her.' We look at each other until he drops his eyes. He drops his eyes, and I know I've won.

Dad's always saying the bigger they are, the harder they fall. I've never had reason to believe any of his silly sayings, until now.

I turn my back on yesterday's news, elated but still weak. I just can't stop my hands from shaking, so I ball them into tight fists instead. However, this is only a minor problem in the sea of problems that I still have to face -the first being that dragon.

I don't have a choice. For all my show of bravado there's no way that we'll be allowed to leave the hall without the puzzle being solved. The Purple Lady doesn't say anything, but she doesn't have to. She knows that I know that Win knows that Stupid knows that they have unfinished business. You know, we all know, no one's leaving the hall until we know the answer!

What makes it worse, much worse, is that there is only one chance to get it right – I can't even begin to let my mind wander to what might happen to Arty if I fail. Failure in my book is not an option.

I whisper each word softly to myself.

'It is cloaked in a place where only the Great, with hearts forced full of warmth will have only once chance to find it.'

My mind locks on each word in turn and I realise we've solved it – well, apart from one tiny part, the part that's causing all the trouble.

The crown is hidden in the Great Hall and the warm hearth had led us to reveal the Dragon. Now all I need to do is to force the dragon's heart full of warmth. My eyes snag on the sweet little dragon with a frown. I don't do cute. In fact, I don't have a cute bone in my body. My life is full of facts; there is no room for even a smidgeon of cuteness to creep in. But if I did do cute, I'd have to say that Arty's dragon is the cutest little dragon I've ever seen – and all I have to do is fill his heart with warmth. I slap my head as the answer pings to attention in my brain.

Of course - I have to press the Dragon's heart. Whoop. Easy peasy when you know how. Where on earth does a dragon keep its heart again?

The sweat trickles down my neck, despite the freezing temperatures. The pressure's unbearable. Everything depends on me completing this one last task - this one last task that I only have one chance to get right. I look wildly around for the one person in the room that can help me, hoping that he hasn't decided to do a disappearing act again.

My eyes rest on him as he lounges against the wall, a calm serene expression on his face. I notice for the first time that his cloak is open, revealing his right hand pressing against his tunic - just over where his heart would be, that is if ghosts had hearts. I give him a little nod before turning back to the dragon. With shaking hands, I lift them both over where the dragon's heart should be and press with all my might.

Treasure

For a second, just one second, I close my eyes: I'm dizzy with anticipation and fear - we've been let down too many times in the past for it to be otherwise.

I open them to the sound of a single muffled click, but not like any click I've ever heard before. This is the centuries old sound of rusty metal clunking and churning together. With all eyes on the brick, it starts to move slowly, as if someone's standing behind the wall and pushing it out of the hole. I jump back a few steps, breath caught in my chest, as the stone balances precariously on the edge before toppling out and landing by my feet in a thousand smashed pieces.

Silence follows as we all stare at the neck of the dirty pale brown hessian sack, peeking out of the top of the hole.

I break the silence by shouting across to Win.

'Without you, we'd never have found anything. You're looking first.'

'Me?' his voice cracking. 'Are you sure?'

'Just hurry up, before someone else grabs it.'

I watch, as he weaves his way across the Hall and hope that this will be his turning point - his time to draw a line through the past and think of new beginnings. No matter what's hidden in that dark mysterious gap in the wall, there's no changing the fact that we'd only discovered it because of Win's enthusiasm and brains.

He stands beside me, shoulders straightening and eyes glistening with excitement. I pat him on the back, would you believe it's the first time I've ever touched him?

His hands hover over the bag, almost reverently as if he doesn't want to touch its secrets, like an unopened Santa sack, somehow more magical and mysterious than the reality can ever be. We all watch as he lifts the frayed loot out of its resting place before lowering it to the floor – the only sound to fill the hall being the slight clink of metal on stone.

With all of us concentrating on Win untying the bag, no one is watching Stupid and his mother. I suddenly see her trotting across the room in Win's direction, but I needn't have worried. Arty, no longer lounging, shoots a leg out and she lands on her bottom with a resounding thud. She tries to scrabble to her feet and the confusion written all over her face is quickly mirrored by her son. The reason she can't move is because a still invisible Arty has decided to take a rest – on her legs. I watch her pink piggy face turn pale as he reaches out a hand to move her hair from her face before speaking. I'd suffer the use of the red spoon forever only to know what Arty had decided to whisper against her ear.

The knot finally gives way and I see a glimpse of black metal. Not the shiny silver I was expecting, until I remember that it's probably tarnished black with time. Win lifts it out of the bag and sets it on the floor in front of him.

We all stare at this strange object, the shape of a dragon. It's obviously very old, very dirty and unlike anything I've ever seen before. It appears to have been welded and beaten into the form of a ferocious dragon's head, with ruby red eyes that glitter and gleam in the torchlight. In the front of the dragon's head, where there should have been nostrils, there's a rusty key protruding out of a lock. With a quick glance at me he turns the key and pulls open the lid.

With five pairs of eyes glued to his every movement, he must feel like an insect under a microscope. He sure doesn't take long to examine the contents, before turning and tilting the box so that we can all see what he is seeing – and boy, what a sight.

The box is laden down with layer upon layer of sparkling jewels in an array of rainbow colours. There's clear diamonds, glowing in the light of the torch, more rubies to match the dragon's eyes and sapphires the size of hen's eggs, not to mention a whole pile of other stones I can't even begin to guess at. Win dips his hands inside and allows the cool stones to run through his fingers like sand on the beach. But as he reaches even further to discover what other mysteries are hidden in its depths his hand stills. He throws a brief look at Arty, before pulling out a dark and, it must be said, distinctly dingy looking circlet. It looks like something you'd find in a junkyard, and a down-market junkyard at that. It looks completely out of place and only fit for the bin - that is until I glance across at Arty's beatific face.

Sometimes what's important isn't the shiny stuff.

But before he can lift it out, the noise of running feet invades the silence, echoing and reverberating around the hall. All eyes tear themselves away from the treasure chest to focus on the figures emerging through the doorway, and this is when Arty steps forward. He reaches out, quick as a flash and takes the crown out of Win's hand before hiding it within the worn folds of his cape where it magically fades from sight.

The Beginning

Two months later

I snuggle up in bed and feel a warm glow spreading across my tummy, as if someone has laid a hot water bottle on top of my pyjamas. This must be what happiness feels like. Not the short-lived feeling you get when you score a goal, but the long-lasting kind you get when you know that something great has happened that has the capacity to change you forever.

I'm not afraid any more, just different. I know I'll always be different on the inside, but Arty has helped me to find the confidence that I lacked. The good thing about confidence is that it seems to spread quicker than you can pass on a cold. Of course, the likes of Guillim and his gang were born with buckets full of the stuff, and do you know what? Now Win and I have our own share, we really don't care.

Would you believe we've even been invited to a couple of birthday parties? Although I'm not sure that this isn't more to do with the Daily Mail's article about treasure seeking Welsh boys, but at least it's a start. The rest of the class have all started to exclude Greasy Guillim and, without his henchmen, he's just a small insignificant blot on the Welsh landscape.

It's a cold dark night outside. I can just see the outline of the yellow moon, glowing through the gap in my new curtains. Yeah that's right 'new curtains' to match my new duvet cover, and not Star Wars either. I'm still not one-hundred-percent convinced of sleeping under a picture of the castle, but Mum's adamant as they were a gift from her boss. She's even been given a pay rise on the back of the huge increase in visitor numbers, although most are either treasure hunters or ghost spotters – neither of which are big spenders in the gift shop.

However, all the news isn't good news but I'm learning that that's normal – as long as there's some sunlight peeking between the clouds, Win and I will be alright. When I came home from school yesterday, I found Arty sprawled across his castle, but not for much longer. He said he wanted to hang around for a couple of months just to make sure I could manage without him. But I think he just likes it here. There's no draughts and no visitors to annoy him but, between you and me, that's not the real reason. He's decided he's a huge Arsenal fan, which, of course, causes ructions as Dad has supported Man U for like centuries.

My eyelids are starting to droop, but I still want to stay awake for a bit longer to relive today. I don't want to ever forget, even a moment.

After what seemed like forever nagging on our part, Mum and Dad finally agreed that Gwen's crown should be returned to its rightful owner. Better that than being kept in some grey museum cabinet gathering dust and never seeing daylight. We all climbed into the back of Dad's old estate car with Gwen's crown wrapped in one of mum's old towels. The mood was buoyant, for everyone apart from me, that is.

I just couldn't stop worrying, but that's part and parcel of my condition. Dad says I think too much – yeah, right. If he thought more, he'd realise what a fright he looked in those trousers. Mum's told him if she finds them in the washing basket she's going to put them in Robin's basket for him to puke all over! Way to go Mum.

Of course, it took us longer than normal people to find our destination. With no Sat Nav to speak of, Dad had to rely on Mum's navigation - not to be recommended at the best of times, and this wasn't the best of times because of those trousers.

Once we'd arrived in Pointon, it didn't take us long to find Gwenllian's final resting place. The long dirt track did cause some annoyance as Dad was wearing his white golfing shoes but, after all this time, I don't think a bit of mud would have worried the Princess. We found her memorial sheltered under a tree bower and enfolded within the arms of a bridge, as if to protect her from further threat. Although what that threat could be, apart from the odd seagull, beats me. What happened to her happened a very long time ago, and something as insignificant as seagull poo could never take away her importance to Welsh history. It's left to us, a very unimportant family from North Wales and a very old ghost, to fit the last piece into the puzzle.

All is quiet, with even the birds remaining silent as Win and I stand side by side, staring at the cold hard ground. Arty is close by, his thoughts hidden by a watery smile. I have to admit that my eyes did feel distinctly damp when I placed the crown on the cold damp earth, and covered it over with the loose stone-free soil.

Boys shouldn't cry, or that's what my dad says. Mum says that if Dad was in tune with his feelings a bit more, he'd know what a prat he looks in those yellow check trousers! I say, it's okay to feel emotional and cry a little, but only at a time and a place of my choosing and not when it's foisted on me by the will of others.

There is no magic present in the shady glade, unless you can call the sense of contentment that invaded our little group magic. I'd like to say the crown just disappeared as soon as it was placed on the ground, but that would make this into a fairy-tale.

If this was a fairy-tale don't you think I'd have chosen to be the tall dark handsome prince, instead of the short, geeky, red-haired be-speckled nerd with Asperger's?

Well, you'd be wrong. My hair's auburn, not red. My mum says my eyes can be fixed if I want when I'm older and I've grown at least two millimetres in the last month. And as for having Asperger's – I view having Asperger's in the same light as the Welsh weather. There's no point in beating myself up about something I can't change and I quite like the rain.

The mists of sleep crowd in and finally start to win. My last thought is of Win and me. Gwen's story is now over, but ours is only just beginning.

The End, but it doesn't have to be...

See you around

Dai

Fab Facts

Q. So did King Arthur Exist?

A. The honest answer is I don't know. But King Arthur's Crown did!

Q. What????

A. King Edward 1 invaded Wales in the Thirteenth Century, building many castles including Conwy Castle, which is featured in this book. When he defeated the Welsh King in 1282 he sent 'Coron Arthur,' or King Arthur's crown to be presented at Westminster Abbey. It ended up being stored in the Tower of London along with the crown jewels.

Q. So where's it now?

A. Well, no one knows. I'd like to think that one day it will turn up, but who knows.

Want to know more about the true origins of the legend of King Arthur? Ask a parent, guardian or teacher to help you find information on the following two people as they hold the answer.

Geoffrey of Mommouth

Nennius

Both sadly lived many hundreds of years ago, but is it a coincidence that they were both Welsh?

For more on Princess Gwenllian please visit her very own website: http://www.princessgwenllian.co.uk/

For more on Dai Monday – Why not catch his next book?

Granny's Gone AWOL in Guernsey…

Jenny O'B

Reference 'A Great and Terrible King: Edward 1 and the forging of Britain,' Marc Morris, 2009

JENNY O'BRIEN

Note for grown-ups

This has been professionally edited to UK English by the amazing Natasha Orme.

My children's books are not for profit. Boy Brainy is available for free, as an ebook on Amazon and other outlets, while the follow-up book in this series, Granny's Gone AWOL in Guernsey is a fundraiser for Ernie's Angels, a local Guernsey charity that supports children with life-limiting conditions.

If you enjoyed this book please pop along to Amazon with some feedback. It really does make a difference. For more on Ernie's Angels and what the charity gets up to please visit their Facebook page on www.facebook.com/erniesangelsguernsey/

Thank you

Jenny O'B

Printed in Great Britain
by Amazon